A Legacy Library Facsimile

JACKANAPES

TOGETHER WITH

DADDY DARWIN'S DOVECOT

AND

LOB LIE-BY-THE-FIRE

By Juliana Horatia Ewing

WITH ILLUSTRATIONS BY

Randolph Caldecott

*As published in London in 1884
by the Society for Promoting Christian Knowledge*

XEROX

UNIVERSITY MICROFILMS, INC.

ANN ARBOR · 1966

J

118139

FROM THE EDITOR
TO THE READER

WE AT LEGACY LIBRARY *had just decided to include* Jackanapes and Other Stories *in our First Series when I ran across an article entitled "Who Reads Mrs. Ewing?" Now this has a rather negative sound and I was tempted to by-pass the article lest it cause me to doubt my editorial judgment. I need not have worried. The whole tenor of the piece was that not nearly enough people read the books of Juliana Horatia Ewing. And that those who don't are missing a rare experience.*

Mrs. Ewing was born in Yorkshire, England, in 1841. Her family was a large one and its members were "literary" in a happily unaffected way. Her father was Vicar of Ecclesfield and a modest scholar and author. Her mother wrote children's books and edited Aunt Judy's Magazine. *Juliana composed plays for the family to present, and served as the household storyteller.*

She grew up to write a dozen books, the best known of which is Jackanapes. *This story and* Daddy Darwin's Dovecot *and* Lob Lie-by-the-Fire *which appear with it in this volume are the only* ones to be illustrated by Caldecott. Their partnership came too late, for both were slated to die much too young. Had they lived longer they almost certainly would have produced much more together for they shared many interests. The English countryside, children, dogs, horses and birds: all that tempted Mrs. Ewing's pen met ready graphic response from Caldecott.

If Mrs. Ewing's early life presaged her later career that of Randolph Caldecott certainly did not. While he was interested in drawing from the time he was six, his family saw no future in an art career and at fifteen he was put to work in a bank. He managed to get some sporadic art training but it was only after twelve years as a bank clerk that he was able to devote much time to his art career.

Once started as an illustrator he became a truly prolific one. His books found quick acceptance, particularly his delightful series of colorful little Picture Books. Unfortunately his never robust health failed him and he died in 1886, a few months after his collaborator, Mrs. Ewing. At the time of his death a great critic wrote: "It seems to me that Caldecott's art was of a quality that appears about once in a century."

As a footnote to the shortsightedness of Caldecott's family is the fact that the most coveted prize in the world of book illustration today is known as the Caldecott Medal.

G. H.

JACKANAPES.

DADDY DARWIN'S DOVECOT.

LOB LIE-BY-THE-FIRE.

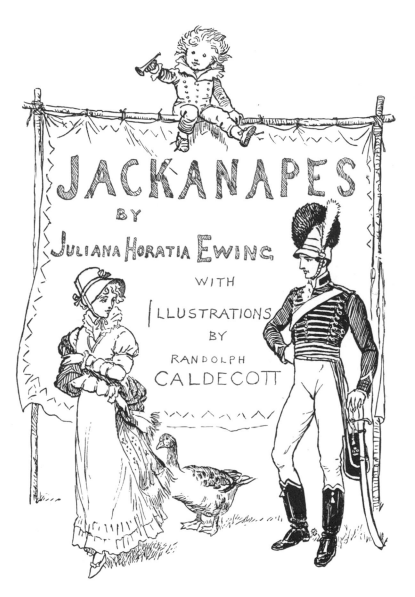

JACKANAPES

BY

JULIANA HORATIA EWING

WITH

ILLUSTRATIONS

BY

RANDOLPH CALDECOTT

LONDON

S.P.C.K., NORTHUMBERLAND AVENUE, W.C.

NEW YORK: E. & J. B. YOUNG & CO.

"If I might buffet for my love, or bound my horse for her favours, I could lay on like a butcher, and sit like a Jackanapes, never off!"

KING HENRY V., Act v., Scene 2.

CHAPTER I.

LAST noon beheld them full of lusty life,
Last eve in Beauty's circle proudly gay,
The midnight brought the signal sound of strife,
The morn the marshalling in arms—the day
Battle's magnificently stern array!
The thunder-clouds close o'er it, which when rent
The earth is covered thick with other clay,
Which her own clay shall cover, heaped and pent,
Rider and horse.—friend, foe,—in one red burial blent.

Their praise is hymn'd by loftier harps than mine:
Yet one would I select from that proud throng.
——to thee, to thousands, of whom each
And one as all a ghastly gap did make
In his own kind and kindred, whom to teach
Forgetfulness were mercy for their sake;
The Archangel's trump, not glory's, must awake
Those whom they thirst for.—BYRON.

TWO Donkeys and the Geese lived on the Green, and all other residents of any social standing lived in houses round it. The houses had no names. Everybody's address was, "The Green," but the Postman and the people of the place knew where each family lived. As to the rest of the world, what has one to do with the rest of the world, when he is safe at home on his own Goose Green? Moreover, if a stranger did come on any lawful business, he might ask his way at the shop.

Most of the inhabitants were long-lived, early deaths
(like that of the little Miss Jessamine) being exceptional;
and most of the old people were proud of their age, especially the sexton, who would be ninety-nine come Martin-
mas, and whose father remembered a man who had carried
arrows, as a boy, for the battle of Flodden Field. The
Grey Goose and the big Miss Jessamine were the only
elderly persons who kept their ages secret. Indeed, Miss
Jessamine never mentioned any one's age, or recalled the
exact year in which anything had happened. She said
that she had been taught that it was bad manners to do so
" in a mixed assembly."

The Grey Goose also avoided dates, but this was partly
because her brain, though intelligent, was not mathe-
matical, and computation was beyond her. She never got
farther than "last Michaelmas," "the Michaelmas before
that," and "the Michaelmas before the Michaelmas before
that." After this her head, which was small, became confused, and she said, " Ga, ga!" and changed the subject.

But she remembered the little Miss Jessamine, the Miss
Jessamine with the "conspicuous" hair. Her aunt, the big
Miss Jessamine, said it was her only fault. The hair was
clean, was abundant, was glossy, but do what you would
with it it never looked quite like other people's. And at
church, after Saturday night's wash, it shone like the best
brass fender after a Spring cleaning. In short, it was
conspicuous, which does not become a young woman—
especially in church.

Those were worrying times altogether, and the Green
was used for strange purposes. A political meeting was
held on it with the village Cobbler in the chair, and a
speaker who came by stage coach from the town, where
they had wrecked the bakers' shops, and discussed the
price of bread. He came a second time, by stage, but the
people had heard something about him in the meanwhile,

and they did not keep him on the Green. They took him to the pond and tried to make him swim, which he could not do, and the whole affair was very disturbing to all quiet and peaceable fowls. After which another man came, and preached sermons on the Green, and a great many people went to hear him ; for those were "trying times," and folk ran hither and thither for comfort. And then what did they do but drill the ploughboys on the Green, to get them ready to fight the French, and teach them the goose-step! However, that came to an end at last, for Bony was sent to St. Helena, and the ploughboys were sent back to the plough.

Everybody lived in fear of Bony in those days, especially the naughty children, who were kept in order during the day by threats of, " Bony shall have you," and who had nightmares about him in the dark. They thought he was an Ogre in a cocked hat. The Grey Goose thought he was a Fox, and that all the men of England were going out in red coats to hunt him. It was no use to argue the point, for she had a very small head, and when one idea got into it there was no room for another.

Besides, the Grey Goose never saw Bony, nor did the children, which rather spoilt the terror of him, so that the Black Captain became more effective as a Bogy with hardened offenders. The Grey Goose remembered *his* coming to the place perfectly. What he came for she did not pretend to know. It was all part and parcel of the war and bad times. He was called the Black Captain, partly because of himself, and partly because of his wonderful black mare. Strange stories were afloat of how far and how fast that mare could go, when her master's hand was on her mane and he whispered in her ear. Indeed, some people thought we might reckon ourselves very lucky if we were not out of the frying-pan into the fire, and had not got a certain well-known Gentleman of the Road to protect us against the French. But that, of course, made him none the less useful to the Johnsons' Nurse, when the little Miss Johnsons were naughty.

"You leave off crying this minnit, Miss Jane, or I'll give you right away to that horrid wicked officer. Jemima! just look out o' the windy, if you please, and see if the Black Cap'n's a-coming with his horse to carry away Miss Jane."

And there, sure enough, the Black Captain strode by, with his sword clattering as if it did not know whose head to cut off first. But he did not call for Miss Jane that time. He went on to the Green, where he came so suddenly upon the eldest Master Johnson, sitting in a puddle on purpose, in his new nankeen skeleton suit, that the young gentleman thought judgment had overtaken him at last, and abandoned himself to the howlings of despair. His howls were redoubled when he was clutched from behind and swung over the Black Captain's shoulder, but in five minutes his tears were stanched, and he was playing with the officer's accoutrements. All of which the Grey Goose saw with her own eyes, and heard afterwards that that bad boy had been whining to go back to the Black Captain ever since, which showed how hardened he was, and that nobody but Bonaparte himself could be expected to do him any good.

But those were "trying times." It was bad enough when the pickle of a large and respectable family cried for the Black Captain; when it came to the little Miss Jessamine crying for him, one felt that the sooner the French landed and had done with it the better.

The big Miss Jessamine's objection to him was that he was a soldier, and this prejudice was shared by all the Green. "A soldier," as the speaker from the town had observed, "is a bloodthirsty, unsettled sort of a rascal; that the peaceable, home-loving, bread-winning citizen can never conscientiously look on as a brother, till he has beaten his sword into a ploughshare, and his spear into a pruninghook."

On the other hand there was some truth in what the Postman (an old soldier) said in reply ; that the sword has to cut a way for us out of many a scrape into which our bread-winners get us when they drive their ploughshares into fallows that don't belong to them.   Indeed, whilst our most peaceful citizens were prosperous chiefly by means of cotton, of sugar, and of the rise and fall of the money-market (not to speak of such saleable matters as opium, firearms, and "black ivory"), disturbances were apt to arise in India, Africa and other outlandish parts, where the fathers of our domestic race were making fortunes for their families.   And, for that matter, even on the Green, we did not wish the military to leave us in the lurch, so long as there was any fear that the French were coming.*

To let the Black Captain have little Miss Jessamine, however, was another matter.   Her Aunt would not hear of it ; and then, to crown all, it appeared that the Captain's father did not think the young lady good enough for his son.   Never was any affair more clearly brought to a conclusion.

But those were "trying times ;" and one moonlight night, when the Grey Goose was sound asleep upon one leg, the Green was rudely shaken under her by the thud of a horse's feet.   "Ga, ga!" said she, putting down the other leg, and running away.

By the time she returned to her place not a thing was

---

* "The political men declare war, and generally for commercial interests ; but when the nation is thus embroiled with its neighbours the soldier . . . draws the sword, at the command of his country. . . . One word as to thy comparison of military and commercial persons. What manner of men be they who have supplied the Caffres with the firearms and ammunition to maintain their savage and deplorable wars ? Assuredly they are not military. . . . Cease then, if thou would'st be counted among the just, to vilify soldiers."—W. NAPIER, Lieut.-General, *November*, 1851.

to be seen or heard. The horse had passed like a shot.
But next day, there was hurrying and skurrying and
cackling at a very early hour, all about the white house
with the black beams, where Miss Jessamine lived. And
when the sun was so low, and the shadows so long on the
grass that the Grey Goose felt ready to run away at the
sight of her own neck, little Miss Jane Johnson, and her
"particular friend" Clarinda, sat under the big oak-tree on
the Green, and Jane pinched Clarinda's little finger till she

found that she could keep a secret, and then she told her
in confidence that she had heard from Nurse and Jemima
that Miss Jessamine's niece had been a very naughty girl,
and that that horrid wicked officer had come for her on his
black horse, and carried her right away.

"Will she never come back?" asked Clarinda.

"Oh, no!" said Jane decidedly. "Bony never brings
people back."

"Not never no more?" sobbed Clarinda, for she was weak-minded, and could not bear to think that Bony never never let naughty people go home again.

Next day Jane had heard more.

"He has taken her to a Green."

"A Goose Green?" asked Clarinda.

"No. A Gretna Green. Don't ask so many questions, child," said Jane; who, having no more to tell, gave herself airs.

Jane was wrong on one point. Miss Jessamine's niece did come back, and she and her husband were forgiven. The Grey Goose remembered it well, it was Michaelmas-tide, the Michaelmas before the Michaelmas before the Michaelmas—but, ga, ga! What does the date matter? It was autumn, harvest-time, and everybody was so busy prophesying and praying about the crops, that the young couple wandered through the lanes, and got blackberries for Miss Jessamine's celebrated crab and blackberry jam, and made guys of themselves with bryony-wreaths, and not a soul troubled his head about them, except the children, and the Postman. The children dogged the Black Captain's footsteps (his bubble reputation as an Ogre having burst), clamouring for a ride on the black mare. And the Postman would go somewhat out of his postal way to catch the Captain's dark eye, and show that he had not forgotten how to salute an officer.

But they were "trying times." One afternoon the black mare was stepping gently up and down the grass, with her head at her master's shoulder, and as many children crowded on to her silky back as if she had been an elephant in a menagerie; and the next afternoon she carried him away, sword and *sabre-tache* clattering war-music at her side, and the old Postman waiting for them, rigid with salutation, at the four cross roads.

War and bad times! It was a hard winter, and the

big Miss Jessamine and the little Miss Jessamine (but she was Mrs. Black-Captain now), lived very economically that they might help their poorer neighbours.   They neither entertained nor went into company, but the young lady

always went up the village as far as the *George and Dragon*, for air and exercise, when the London Mail* came in.

* The Mail Coach it was that distributed over the face of the land, like the opening of apocalyptic vials, the heart-shaking news of Trafalgar, of Salamanca, of Vittoria, of Waterloo. . . . The grandest chapter of our experience, within the whole Mail Coach service, was on those occasions when we went down from London with the news of Victory. Five years of life it was worth paying down for the privilege of an outside place.

DE QUINCEY.

One day (it was a day in the following June) it came in earlier than usual, and the young lady was not there to meet it.

But a crowd soon gathered round the *George and Dragon*, gaping to see the Mail Coach dressed with flowers and oak-leaves, and the guard wearing a laurel wreath over and above his royal livery. The ribbons that decked the horses were stained and flecked with the warmth and foam of the pace at which they had come, for they had pressed on with the news of Victory.

Miss Jessamine was sitting with her niece under the oak-tree on the Green, when the Postman put a newspaper silently into her hand. Her niece turned quickly—

"Is there news?"

"Don't agitate yourself, my dear," said her aunt. "I will read it aloud, and then we can enjoy it together; a far more comfortable method, my love, than when you go up the village, and come home out of breath, having snatched half the news as you run."

"I am all attention, dear aunt," said the little lady, clasping her hands tightly on her lap.

Then Miss Jessamine read aloud—she was proud of her reading—and the old soldier stood at attention behind her, with such a blending of pride and pity on his face as it was strange to see :—   "DOWNING STREET,
                                   June 22, 1815, I A.M."

"That's one in the morning," gasped the Postman; "beg your pardon, mum."

But though he apologised, he could not refrain from echoing here and there a weighty word. "Glorious victory,"—"Two hundred pieces of artillery,"—"Immense quantity of ammunition,"—and so forth.

" The loss of the British Army upon this occasion has unfortunately been most severe. It had not been possible to make out a return of the killed and wounded when Major Percy left headquarters. The names of the officers killed and wounded, as far as they can be collected, are annexed.
                              "I have the honour——"

"The list, aunt!   Read the list!"

"My love—my darling—let us go in and——"

"No.   Now! now!"

To one thing the supremely afflicted are entitled in their sorrow—to be obeyed—and yet it is the last kindness that people commonly will do them.   But Miss Jessamine did.   Steadying her voice, as best she might, she read on, and the old soldier stood bareheaded to hear that first Roll of the Dead at Waterloo, which began with the Duke of Brunswick, and ended with Ensign Brown.*   Five-and thirty British Captains fell asleep that day on the bed of Honour, and the Black Captain slept among them.

*   *   *   *   *   *

There are killed and wounded by war, of whom no returns reach Downing Street.

Three days later, the Captain's wife had joined him, and Miss Jessamine was kneeling by the cradle of their orphan son, a purple-red morsel of humanity, with conspicuously golden hair.

"Will he live, Doctor?"

"Live?   GOD bless my soul, ma'am!   Look at him!   The young Jackanapes!"

---

* "Brunswick's fated chieftain" fell at Quatre Bras, the day before Waterloo, but this first (very imperfect) list, as it appeared in the newspapers of the day, did begin with his name, and end with that of an Ensign Brown.

CHAPTER II.

And he wandered away and away
With Nature, the dear old Nurse.
                    LONGFELLOW.

HE Grey Goose remembered quite well the year that Jackanapes began to walk, for it was the year that the speckled hen for the first time in all her motherly life got out of patience when she was sitting. She had been rather proud of the eggs—they were unusually large—but she never felt quite comfortable on them ; and whether it was because she used to get cramp, and go off the nest, or because the season was bad, or what, she never could tell, but every egg was addled but one, and the one that did hatch gave her more trouble than any chick she had ever reared.

It was a fine, downy, bright yellow little thing, but it had a monstrous big nose and feet, and such an ungainly walk as she knew no other instance of in her well-bred and high-stepping family. And as to behaviour, it was not that it was either quarrelsome or moping, but simply unlike the rest. When the other chicks hopped and cheeped on the Green about their mother's feet, this solitary yellow brat went waddling off on its own responsibility, and do or cluck what the speckled hen would, it went to play in the pond.

It was off one day as usual, and the hen was fussing

and fuming after it, when the Postman, going to deliver a
letter at Miss Jessamine's door, was nearly knocked over
by the good lady herself, who, bursting out of the house
with her cap just off and her bonnet just not on, fell into
his arms, crying—

"Baby! Baby! Jackanapes! Jackanapes!"

If the Postman loved anything on earth, he loved the

Captain's yellowed-haired child, so propping Miss Jessamine against her own door-post, he followed the direction
of her trembling fingers and made for the Green.

Jackanapes had had the start of the Postman by nearly
ten minutes. The world—the round green world with an
oak tree on it—was just becoming very interesting to him.
He had tried, vigorously but ineffectually, to mount a

passing pig the last time he was taken out walking ; but then he was encumbered with a nurse. Now he was his own master, and might, by courage and energy, become the master of that delightful, downy, dumpy, yellow thing, that was bobbing along over the green grass in front of him. Forward ! Charge ! He aimed well, and grabbed it, but only to feel the delicious downiness and dumpiness slipping through his fingers as he fell upon his face. " Quawk ! " said the yellow thing, and wobbled off sideways. It was this oblique movement that enabled Jackanapes to come up with it, for it was bound for the Pond, and therefore obliged to come back into line. He failed again from top-heaviness, and his prey escaped sideways as before, and, as before, lost ground in getting back to the direct road to the Pond.

And at the Pond the Postman found them both, one yellow thing rocking safely on the ripples that lie beyond duck-weed, and the other washing his draggled frock with tears, because he too had tried to sit upon the Pond, and it wouldn't hold him.

CHAPTER III.

. . . If studious, copie fair what time hath blurred,
Redeem truth from his jawes ; if souldier,
Chase brave employments with a naked sword
Throughout the world.   Fool not ; for all may have,
If they dare try, a glorious life, or grave.
   *   *   *   *   *
In brief, acquit thee bravely : play the man.
Look not on pleasures as they come, but go.
Defer not the least vertue : life's poore span
Make not an ell, by trifling in thy woe.
If thou do ill, the joy fades, not the pains.
If well : the pain doth fade, the joy remains.

GEORGE HERBERT.

OUNG Mrs. Johnson, who was a mother of many, hardly knew which to pity more ; Miss Jessamine for having her little ways and her antimacassars rumpled by a young Jackanapes ; or the boy himself, for being brought up by an old maid.

Oddly enough, she would probably have pitied neither, had Jackanapes been a girl. (One is so apt to think that what works smoothest works to the highest ends, having no patience for the results of friction.) That Father in GOD, who bade the young men to be pure, and the maidens brave, greatly disturbed a member of his congregation, who thought that the great preacher had made a slip of the tongue.

" That the girls should have purity, and the boys courage, is what you would say, good Father ? "

" Nature has done that," was the reply ; " I meant what I said."

In good sooth, a young maid is all the better for learning some robuster virtues than maidenliness and not to move the antimacassars. And the robuster virtues require some fresh air and freedom. As, on the other hand, Jackanapes (who had a boy's full share of the little beast and the young monkey in his natural composition) was none the worse, at his tender years, for learning some maidenliness —so far as maidenliness means decency, pity, unselfishness and pretty behaviour.

And it is due to' him to say that he was an obedient boy, and a boy whose word could be depended on, long before his grandfather the General came to live at the Green.

He was obedient ; that is he did what his great aunt told him. But—oh dear! oh dear !—the pranks he played, which it had never entered into her head to forbid !

It was when he had just been put into skeletons (frocks never suited him) that he became very friendly with Master Tony Johnson, a younger brother of the young gentleman who sat in the puddle on purpose. Tony was not enterprising, and Jackanapes led him by the nose. One summer's evening they were out late, and Miss Jessamine was becoming anxious, when Jackanapes presented himself with a ghastly face all besmirched with tears. He was unusually subdued.

" I'm afraid," he sobbed ; " if you please, I'm very much afraid that Tony Johnson's dying in the churchyard."

Miss Jessamine was just beginning to be distracted, when she smelt Jackanapes.

" You naughty, naughty boys ! Do you mean to tell me that you've been smoking ? "

" Not pipes," urged Jackanapes ; " upon my honour, Aunty, not pipes. Only segars like Mr. Johnson's ! and only made of brown paper with a very very little tobacco from the shop inside them."

Whereupon, Miss Jessamine sent a servant to the churchyard, who found Tony Johnson lying on a tombstone, very sick, and having ceased to entertain any hopes of his own recovery.

If it could be possible that any "unpleasantness" could arise between two such amiable neighbours as Miss Jessamine and Mrs. Johnson—and if the still more incredible paradox can be that ladies may differ over a point on which they are agreed—that point was the admitted fact that Tony Johnson was "delicate," and the difference lay chiefly in this : Mrs. Johnson said that Tony was delicate— meaning that he was more finely strung, more sensitive, a properer subject for pampering and petting than Jackanapes, and that, consequently, Jackanapes was to blame for leading Tony into scrapes which resulted in his being chilled, frightened, or (most frequently) sick. But when Miss Jessamine said that Tony Johnson was delicate, she meant that he was more puling, less manly, and less healthily brought up than Jackanapes, who, when they got into mischief together, was certainly not to blame because his friend could not get wet, sit a kicking donkey, ride in the giddy-go-round, bear the noise of a cracker, or smoke brown paper with impunity, as he could.

Not that there was ever the slightest quarrel between the ladies. It never even came near it, except the day after Tony had been so very sick with riding Bucephalus in the giddy-go-round. Mrs. Johnson had explained to Miss Jessamine that the reason Tony was so easily upset, was the unusual sensitiveness (as a doctor had explained it

to her) of the nervous centres in her family—" Fiddlestick!"
So Mrs. Johnson understood Miss Jessamine to say, but it
appeared that she only said "Treaclestick!" which is quite
another thing, and of which Tony was undoubtedly fond.

It was at the fair that Tony was made ill by riding on
Bucephalus. Once a year the Goose Green became the
scene of a carnival. First of all, carts and caravans were
rumbling up all along, day and night. Jackanapes could
hear them as he lay in bed, and could hardly sleep for
speculating what booths and whirligigs he should find
fairly established, when he and his dog Spitfire went out
after breakfast. As a matter of fact, he seldom had to
wait so long for news of the Fair. The Postman knew the
window out of which Jackanapes' yellow head would come,
and was ready with his report.

"Royal Theayter, Master Jackanapes, in the old place,
but be careful o' them seats, sir ; they're rickettier than
ever. Two sweets and a ginger-beer under the oak tree,
and the Flying Boats is just a-coming along the road."

No doubt it was partly because he had already suffered
severely in the Flying Boats, that Tony collapsed so
quickly in the giddy-go-round. He only mounted Bucephalus (who was spotted, and had no tail,) because Jackanapes urged him, and held out the ingenious hope that the
round-and-round feeling would very likely cure the up-and-
down sensation. It did not, however, and Tony tumbled
off during the first revolution.

Jackanapes was not absolutely free from qualms, but
having once mounted the Black Prince he stuck to him as
a horseman should. During the first round he waved his
hat, and observed with some concern that the Black Prince
had lost an ear since last Fair ; at the second, he looked a
little pale, but sat upright, though somewhat unnecessarily
rigid ; at the third round he shut his eyes. During the
fourth his hat fell off, and he clasped his horse's neck. By

the fifth he had laid his yellow head against the Black Prince's mane, and so clung anyhow till the hobby-horses stopped, when the proprietor assisted him to alight, and he sat down rather suddenly and said he had enjoyed it very much.

The Grey Goose always ran away at the first approach of the caravans, and never came back to the Green till there was nothing left of the Fair but footmarks and oyster-shells. Running away was her pet principle; the only system, she maintained, by which you can live long and easily, and lose nothing. If you run away when you see danger, you can come back when all is safe. Run quickly, return slowly, hold your head high, and gabble as loud as you can, and you'll preserve the respect of the Goose Green to a peaceful old age. Why should you struggle and get hurt, if you can lower your head and swerve, and not lose a feather? Why in the world should any one spoil the pleasure of life, or risk his skin, if he can help it?

"'What's the use?'
Said the Goose."

Before answering which one might have to consider what
world—which life—and whether his skin were a goose-
skin; but the Grey Goose's head would never have held
all that.

Grass soon grows over footprints, and the village children took the oyster-shells to trim their gardens with;
but the year after Tony rode Bucephalus there lingered
another relic of Fair-time, in which Jackanapes was deeply
interested. "The Green" proper was originally only part
of a straggling common, which in its turn merged into
some wilder waste land where gipsies sometimes squatted
if the authorities would allow them, especially after the
annual Fair. And it was after the Fair that Jackanapes,
out rambling by himself, was knocked over by the Gipsy's
son riding the Gipsy's red-haired pony at break-neck pace
across the common.

Jackanapes got up and shook himself, none the worse,
except for being heels over head in love with the red-haired
pony. What a rate he went at! How he spurned the
ground with his nimble feet! How his red coat shone in
the sunshine! And what bright eyes peeped out of his
dark forelock as it was blown by the wind!

The Gipsy boy had had a fright, and he was willing
enough to reward Jackanapes for not having been hurt, by
consenting to let him have a ride.

"Do you mean to kill the little fine gentleman, and
swing us all on the gibbet, you rascal?" screamed the
Gipsy-mother, who came up just as Jackanapes and the
pony set off.

"He would get on," replied her son. "It'll not kill him.
He'll fall on his yellow head, and it's as tough as a cocoa-
nut."

But Jackanapes did not fall. He stuck to the red-
haired pony as he had stuck to the hobby-horse; but oh,
how different the delight of this wild gallop with flesh and

blood! Just as his legs were beginning to feel as if he did not feel them, the Gipsy boy cried "Lollo!" Round went the pony so unceremoniously, that, with as little ceremony, Jackanapes clung to his neck, and he did not properly recover himself before Lollo stopped with a jerk at the place where they had started.

"Is his name Lollo?" asked Jackanapes, his hand lingering in the wiry mane.

"Yes."

"What does Lollo mean?"

"Red."

"Is Lollo your pony?"

"No. My father's." And the Gipsy boy led Lollo away.

At the first opportunity Jackanapes stole away again to the common. This time he saw the Gipsy-father, smoking a dirty pipe.

"Lollo is your pony, isn't he?" said Jackanapes.

"Yes."

"He's a very nice one."

"He's a racer."

"You don't want to sell him, do you?"

"Fifteen pounds," said the Gipsy-father; and Jackanapes sighed and went home again. That very afternoon he and Tony rode the two donkeys, and Tony managed to get thrown, and even Jackanapes' donkey kicked. But it was jolting, clumsy work after the elastic swiftness and the dainty mischief of the red-haired pony.

A few days later Miss Jessamine spoke very seriously to Jackanapes. She was a good deal agitated as she told him that his grandfather the General was coming to the Green, and that he must be on his very best behaviour during the visit. If it had been feasible to leave off calling him Jackanapes and to get used to his baptismal name of Theodore before the day after to-morrow (when

the General was due), it would have been satisfactory.
But Miss Jessamine feared it would be impossible in practice, and she had scruples about it on principle. It would
not seem quite truthful, although she had always most
fully intended that he should be called Theodore when he
had outgrown the ridiculous appropriateness of his nick-
name. The fact was that he had not outgrown it, but he
must take care to remember who was meant when his
grandfather said Theodore.

Indeed for that matter he must take care all along.

"You are apt to be giddy, Jackanapes," said Miss
Jessamine.

"Yes aunt," said Jackanapes, thinking of the hobby-
horses.

"You are a good boy, Jackanapes. Thank GOD, I can
tell your grandfather that. An obedient boy, an honourable boy, and a kind-hearted boy. But you are—in short,
you *are* a Boy, Jackanapes. And I hope"—added Miss
Jessamine, desperate with the results of experience—"that
the General knows that Boys will be Boys."

What mischief could be foreseen, Jackanapes promised
to guard against. He was to keep his clothes and his
hands clean, to look over his catechism, not to put sticky
things in his pockets, to keep that hair of his smooth—
("It's the wind that blows it, Aunty," said Jackanapes—
"I'll send by the coach for some bear's-grease," said Miss
Jessamine, tying a knot in her pocket-handkerchief)—not
to burst in at the parlour door, not to talk at the top
of his voice, not to crumple his Sunday frill, and to sit
quite quiet during the sermon, to be sure to say "sir" to
the General, to be careful about rubbing his shoes on the
door-mat, and to bring his lesson-books to his aunt at once
that she might iron down the dogs' ears. The General
arrived, and for the first day all went well, except that
Jackanapes' hair was as wild as usual, for the hairdresser

had no bear's grease left. He began to feel more at ease with his grandfather, and disposed to talk confidentially with him, as he did with the Postman. All that the General felt it would take too long to tell, but the result was the same. He was disposed to talk confidentially with Jackanapes.

"Mons'ous pretty place this," he said, looking out of

the lattice on to the Green, where the grass was vivid with sunset, and the shadows were long and peaceful.

"You should see it in Fair-week, sir," said Jackanapes, shaking his yellow mop, and leaning back in his one of the two Chippendale arm-chairs in which they sat.

"A fine time that, eh?" said the General, with a twinkle in his left eye. (The other was glass.)

Jackanapes shook his hair once more. " I enjoyed this last one the best of all," he said. " I'd so much money."

" By George, it's not a common complaint in these bad times. How much had ye ? "

" I'd two shillings. A new shilling Aunty gave me, and elevenpence I had saved up, and a penny from the Postman—-sir!" added Jackanapes with a jerk, having forgotten it.

" And how did ye spend it—sir ? " inquired the General.

Jackanapes spread his ten fingers on the arms of his chair, and shut his eyes that he might count the more conscientiously.

" Watch-stand for Aunty, threepence. Trumpet for myself, twopence, that's fivepence. Ginger-nuts for Tony, twopence, and a mug with a Grenadier on for the Postman, fourpence, that's elevenpence. Shooting-gallery a penny, that's a shilling. Giddy-go-round, a penny, that's one and a penny. Treating Tony, one and twopence. Flying Boats (Tony paid for himself), a penny, one and threepence. Shooting-gallery again, one and fourpence ; Fat Woman a penny, one and fivepence. Giddy-go-round again, one and sixpence. Shooting-gallery, one and sevenpence. Treating Tony, and then he wouldn't shoot, so I did, one and eight-pence. Living Skeleton, a penny—no, Tony treated me, the Living Skeleton doesn't count. Skittles, a penny, one and ninepence. Mermaid (but when we got inside she was dead), a penny, one and tenpence. Theatre, a penny (Priscilla Partington, or the Green Lane Murder. A beautiful young lady, sir, with pink cheeks and a real pistol), that's one and elevenpence. Ginger beer, a penny (I *was* so thirsty!) two shillings. And then the Shooting-gallery man gave me a turn for nothing, because, he said, I was a real gentleman, and spent my money like a man."

" So you do, sir, so you do ! " cried the General. " Why,

sir, you spend it like a prince. And now I suppose you've
not got a penny in your pocket? "

"Yes I have," said Jackanapes. "Two pennies. They
are saving up." And Jackanapes jingled them with his
hand.

"You don't want money except at fair-times, I suppose?" said the General.

Jackanapes shook his mop.

"If I could have as much as I want, I should know
what to buy," said he.

"And how much do you want, if you could get it?"

"Wait a minute, sir, till I think what twopence from
fifteen pounds leaves. Two from nothing you can't, but
borrow twelve. Two from twelve, ten, and carry one.
Please remember ten, sir, when I ask you. One from
nothing you can't, borrow twenty. One from twenty,
nineteen, and carry one. One from fifteen, fourteen.
Fourteen pounds nineteen and—what did I tell you to
remember? "

"Ten," said the General.

"Fourteen pounds nineteen shillings and tenpence then,
is what I want," said Jackanapes.

"Bless my soul, what for? "

"To buy Lollo with. Lollo means red, sir. The
Gipsy's red-haired pony, sir. Oh, he *is* beautiful! You
should see his coat in the sunshine! You should see his
mane! You should see his tail! Such little feet, sir, and
they go like lightning! Such a dear face, too, and eyes
like a mouse! But he's a racer, and the Gipsy wants
fifteen pounds for him."

"If he's a racer, you couldn't ride him. Could you? "

"No—o, sir, but I can stick to him. I did the other
day."

"You did, did you? Well, I'm fond of riding myself,
and if the beast is as good as you say, he might suit me."

"You're too tall for Lollo, I think," said Jackanapes, measuring his grandfather with his eye.

"I can double up my legs, I suppose. We'll have a look at him to-morrow."

"Don't you weigh a good deal?" asked Jackanapes.

"Chiefly waistcoats," said the General, slapping the breast of his military frock-coat. "We'll have the little racer on the Green the first thing in the morning. Glad you mentioned it, grandson. Glad you mentioned it."

The General was as good as his word. Next morning the Gipsy and Lollo, Miss Jessamine, Jackanapes and his grandfather and his dog Spitfire, were all gathered at one end of the Green in a group, which so aroused the innocent curiosity of Mrs. Johnson, as she saw it from one of her upper windows, that she and the children took their early promenade rather earlier than usual. The General talked to the Gipsy, and Jackanapes fondled Lollo's mane, and did not know whether he should be more glad or miserable if his grandfather bought him.

"Jackanapes!"

"Yes, sir!"

"I've bought Lollo, but I believe you were right. He hardly stands high enough for me. If you can ride him to the other end of the Green, I'll give him to you."

How Jackanapes tumbled on to Lollo's back he never knew. He had just gathered up the reins when the Gipsy-father took him by the arm.

"If you want to make Lollo go fast, my little gentle-man——"

"*I* can make him go!" said Jackanapes, and drawing from his pocket the trumpet he had bought in the fair, he blew a blast both loud and shrill.

Away went Lollo, and away went Jackanapes' hat. His golden hair flew out, an aureole from which his cheeks shone red and distended with trumpeting. Away went

Spitfire, mad with the rapture of the race, and the wind in his silky ears. Away went the geese, the cocks, the hens, and the whole family of Johnson. Lucy clung to her mamma, Jane saved Emily by the gathers of her gown, and Tony saved himself by a somersault.

The Grey Goose was just returning when Jackanapes and Lollo rode back, Spitfire panting behind.

"Good, my little gentleman, good!" said the Gipsy. "You were born to the saddle. You've the flat thigh, the

strong knee, the wiry back, and the light caressing hand, all you want is to learn the whisper. Come here!"

"What was that dirty fellow talking about, grandson?" asked the General.

"I can't tell you, sir. It's a secret."

They were sitting in the window again, in the two Chippendale arm-chairs, the General devouring every line of his grandson's face, with strange spasms crossing his own.

" You must love your aunt very much, Jackanapes ? "

" I do, sir," said Jackanapes warmly.

" And whom do you love next best to your aunt ? "

The ties of blood were pressing very strongly on the General himself, and perhaps he thought of Lollo. But Love is not bought in a day, even with fourteen pounds nineteen shillings and tenpence. Jackanapes answered quite readily, " The Postman."

" Why the Postman ? "

" He knew my father," said Jackanapes, " and he tells me about him, and about his black mare. My father was a soldier, a brave soldier. He died at Waterloo. When I grow up I want to be a soldier too."

" So you shall, my boy. So you shall."

" Thank you, grandfather. Aunty doesn't want me to be a soldier for fear of being killed."

" Bless my life ! Would she have you get into a feather-bed and stay there? Why, you might be killed by a thunderbolt, if you were a butter-merchant !"

" So I might. I shall tell her so. What a funny fellow you are, sir ! I say, do you think my father knew the Gipsy's secret ? The Postman says he used to whisper to his black mare."

" Your father was taught to ride as a child, by one of those horsemen of the East who swoop and dart and wheel about a plain like swallows in autumn. Grandson ! Love me a little too. I can tell you more about your father than the Postman can."

" I do love you," said Jackanapes. " Before you came I was frightened. I'd no notion you were so nice."

" Love me always, boy, whatever I do or leave undone. And—GOD help me—whatever you do or leave undone, I'll love you ! There shall never be a cloud between us for a day ; no, sir, not for an hour. We're imperfect enough, all of us, we needn't be so bitter ; and life is uncertain enough at its safest, we needn't waste its opportunities. Look at me! Here sit I, after a dozen battles and some of the worst climates in the world, and by yonder lych gate lies your mother, who didn't move five miles, I suppose, from your aunt's apron-strings,—dead in her teens ; my golden-haired daughter, whom I never saw."

Jackanapes was terribly troubled.

" Don't cry, grandfather," he pleaded, his own blue eyes round with tears. " I will love you very much, and I will try to be very good. But I should like to be a soldier."

" You shall, my boy, you shall. You've more claims for a commission than you know of. Cavalry, I suppose ; eh, ye young Jackanapes ? Well, well ; if you live to be an honour to your country, this old-heart shall grow young again with pride for you ; and if you die in the service of your country—GOD bless me, it can but break for ye ! "

And beating the region which he said was all waistcoats, as if they stifled him, the old man got up and strode out on to the Green.

CHAPTER IV.

"Greater love hath no man than this, that a man lay down his life for his friends."—JOHN xv. 13.

TWENTY and odd years later the Grey Goose was still alive, and in full possession of her faculties, such as they were. She lived slowly and carefully, and she lived long. So did Miss Jessamine ; but the General was dead.

He had lived on the Green for many years, during which he and the Postman saluted each other with a punctiliousness that it almost drilled one to witness. He would have completely spoiled Jackanapes if Miss

D

Jessamine's conscience would have let him ; otherwise he somewhat dragooned his neighbours, and was as positive about parish matters as a ratepayer about the army. A stormy-tempered, tender-hearted soldier, irritable with the suffering of wounds of which he never spoke, whom all the village followed to his grave with tears.

The General's death was a great shock to Miss Jessamine, and her nephew stayed with her for some little time after the funeral. Then he was obliged to join his regiment, which was ordered abroad.

One effect of the conquest which the General had gained over the affections of the village, was a considerable abatement of the popular prejudice against "the military." Indeed the village was now somewhat importantly represented in the army. There was the General himself, and the Postman, and the Black Captain's tablet in the church, and Jackanapes, and Tony Johnson, and a Trumpeter.

Tony Johnson had no more natural taste for fighting than for riding, but he was as devoted as ever to Jackanapes, and that was how it come about that Mr. Johnson bought him a commission in the same cavalry regiment that the General's grandson (whose commission had been given him by the Iron Duke) was in, and that he was quite content to be the butt of the mess where Jackanapes was the hero ; and that when Jackanapes wrote home to Miss Jessamine, Tony wrote with the same purpose to his mother ; namely, to demand her congratulations that they were on active service at last, and were ordered to the front. And he added a postscript to the effect that she could have no idea how popular Jackanapes was, nor how splendidly he rode the wonderful red charger whom he had named after his old friend Lollo.

*   *   *   *   *   *

"Sound Retire!"

A Boy Trumpeter, grave with the weight of responsibilities and accoutrements beyond his years, and stained, so that his own mother would not have known him, with the sweat and dust of battle, did as he was bid ; and then pushing his trumpet pettishly aside, adjusted his weary legs for the hundredth time to the horse which was a world too big for him, and muttering, " 'Taint a pretty tune," tried to see something of this, his first engagement, before it came to an end.

Being literally in the thick of it, he could hardly have

seen less or known less of what happened in that particular skirmish if he had been at home in England. For many good reasons ; including dust and smoke, and that what attention he dared distract from his commanding officer was pretty well absorbed by keeping his hard-mouthed troop-horse in hand, under pain of execration by his neighbours in the melée. By-and-by, when the newspapers came out, if he could get a look at one before it was thumbed to bits, he would learn that the enemy had appeared from ambush in overwhelming numbers, and that orders had been given to fall back, which was done slowly and in good order, the men fighting as they retired.

Born and bred on the Goose Green, the youngest of Mr. Johnson's gardener's numerous offspring, the boy had given his family "no peace" till they let him "go for a soldier" with Master Tony and Master Jackanapes. They consented at last, with more tears than they shed when an elder son was sent to gaol for poaching, and the boy was perfectly happy in his life, and full of *esprit de corps*. It was this which had been wounded by having to sound retreat for "the young gentlemen's regiment," the first time he served with it before the enemy, and he was also harassed by having completely lost sight of Master Tony. There had been some hard fighting before the backward movement began, and he had caught sight of him once, but not since. On the other hand, all the pulses of his village pride had been stirred by one or two visions of Master Jackanapes whirling about on his wonderful horse. He had been easy to distinguish, since an eccentric blow had bared his head without hurting it, for his close golden mop of hair gleamed in the hot sunshine as brightly as the steel of the sword flashing round it.

Of the missiles that fell pretty thickly, the Boy Trumpeter did not take much notice. First, one can't attend to everything, and his hands were full. Secondly, one gets used to anything. Thirdly, experience soon teaches one, in spite of proverbs, how very few bullets find their billet. Far more unnerving is the mere suspicion of fear or even of anxiety in the human mass around you. The Boy was beginning to wonder if there were any dark reason for the increasing pressure, and whether they would be allowed to move back more quickly, when the smoke in front lifted for a moment, and he could see the plain, and the enemy's line some two hundred yards away.

And across the plain between them, he saw Master Jackanapes galloping alone at the top of Lollo's speed, their faces to the enemy, his golden head at Lollo's ear.

But at this moment noise and smoke seemed to burst out on every side, the officer shouted to, him to sound retire, and between trumpeting and bumping about on his horse, he saw and heard no more of the incidents of his first battle.

Tony Johnson was always unlucky with horses, from the days of the giddy-go-round onwards. On this day—of all days in the year—his own horse was on the sick list, and he had to ride an inferior, ill-conditioned beast, and fell off that, at the very moment when it was a matter of life or death to be able to ride away. The horse fell on him, but struggled up again, and Tony managed to keep hold of it. It was in trying to remount that he discovered, by helplessness and anguish, that one of his legs was crushed and broken, and that no feat of which he was master would get him into the saddle. Not able even to stand alone, awkwardly, agonizingly unable to mount his restive horse, his life was yet so strong within him! And on one side of him rolled the dust and smoke-cloud of his advancing foes, and on the other, that which covered his retreating friends.

He turned one piteous gaze after them, with a bitter twinge, not of reproach, but of loneliness ; and then, dragging himself up by the side of his horse, he turned the other way and drew out his pistol, and waited for the end. Whether he waited seconds or minutes he never knew, before some one gripped him by the arm.

" *Jackanapes ! GOD bless you !* It's my left leg. If you *could* get me on——"

It was like Tony's luck that his pistol went off at his

horse's tail, and made it plunge ; but Jackanapes threw
him across the saddle.

"Hold on anyhow, and stick your spur in. I'll lead
him. Keep your head down, they're firing high."

And Jackanapes laid his head down—to Lollo's ear.

It was when they were fairly off, that a sudden up-
springing of the enemy in all directions had made it
necessary to change the gradual retirement of our force
into as rapid a retreat as possible. And when Jackanapes
became aware of this, and felt the lagging and swerving of
Tony's horse, he began to wish he had thrown his friend
across his own saddle, and left their lives to Lollo.

When Tony became aware of it, several things came
into his head. 1. That the dangers of their ride for life
were now more than doubled. 2. That if Jackanapes and
Lollo were not burdened with him they would undoubtedly
escape. 3. That Jackanapes' life was infinitely valuable,
and his—Tony's—was not. 4. That this—if he could
seize it—was the supremest of all the moments in which
he had tried to assume the virtues which Jackanapes had
by nature ; and that if he could be courageous and unselfish now——

He caught at his own reins and spoke very loud——

"Jackanapes! It won't do. You and Lollo must go
on. Tell the fellows I gave you back to them, with all my
heart. Jackanapes, if you love me, leave me!"

There was a daffodil light over the evening sky in front
of them, and it shone strangely on Jackanapes' hair and
face. He turned with an odd look in his eyes that a vainer
man than Tony Johnson might have taken for brotherly
pride. Then he shook his mop, and laughed at him.

"*Leave you?* To save my skin? No, Tony, not to
save my soul!"

He caught at his own reins and spoke very loud——
"Jackanapes! It won't do. You and Lollo must go on."

CHAPTER V.

Mr. VALIANT *summoned. His will. His last words.*

Then, said he, "I am going to my Father's. . . . My Sword I give to him that shall succeed me in my Pilgrimage, and my Courage and Skill to him that can get it." . . . And as he went down deeper, he said, "Grave, where is thy Victory?"

So he passed over, and all the Trumpets sounded for him on the other side.

BUNYAN'S *Pilgrim's Progress.*

COMING out of a hospital-tent, at headquarters, the sur- geon cannoned against, and rebounded from, another officer; a sallow man, not young, with a face worn more by ungentle expe- riences than by age; with weary eyes that kept their own counsel, iron-grey hair, and a moustache that was as if a raven had laid its wing across his lips and sealed them.

"Well?"

"Beg pardon, Major. Didn't see you. Oh, com- pound fracture and bruises, but it's all right. He'll pull through."

"Thank GOD."

It was probably an involuntary expression, for prayer

and praise were not much in the Major's line, as a jerk of the surgeon's head would have betrayed to an observer. He was a bright little man, with his feelings showing all over him, but with gallantry and contempt of death enough for both sides of his profession ; who took a cool head, a white handkerchief and a case of instruments, where other men went hot-blooded with weapons, and who was the biggest gossip, male or female, of the regiment. Not even the Major's taciturnity daunted him.

"Didn't think he'd as much pluck about him as he has. He'll do all right if he doesn't fret himself into a fever about poor Jackanapes."

"Whom are you talking about?" asked the Major hoarsely.

"Young Johnson. He——"

"What about Jackanapes?"

"Don't you know? Sad business. Rode back for Johnson, and brought him in ; but, monstrous ill-luck, hit as they rode. Left lung——"

"Will he recover?"

"No. Sad business. What a frame—what limbs— what health—and what good looks! Finest young fellow——"

"Where is he?"

"In his own tent," said the surgeon sadly.

The Major wheeled and left him.

*   *   *   *   *   *

"Can I do anything else for you?"

"Nothing, thank you. Except—Major! I wish I could get you to appreciate Johnson."

"This is not an easy moment, Jackanapes."

"Let me tell you, sir—*he* never will—that if he could have driven me from him, he would be lying yonder at this moment, and I should be safe and sound."

The Major laid his hand over his mouth, as if to keep back a wish he would have been ashamed to utter.

"I've known old Tony from a child. He's a fool on impulse, a good man and a gentleman in principle. And he acts on principle, which it's not every—some water, please! Thank you, sir. It's very hot, and yet one's feet get uncommonly cold. Oh, thank you, thank you. He's no fire-eater, but he has a trained conscience and a tender heart, and he'll do his duty when a braver and more selfish man might fail you. But he wants encouragement ; and when I'm gone——"

"He shall have encouragement. You have my word for it. Can I do nothing else ? "

" Yes, Major. A favour."

" Thank you, Jackanapes."

" Be Lollo's master, and love him as well as you can. He's used to it."

"Wouldn't you rather Johnson had him ? "

The blue eyes twinkled in spite of mortal pain.

" Tony *rides* on principle, Major. His legs are bolsters, and will be to the end of the chapter. I couldn't insult dear Lollo, but if you don't care——"

" Whilst I live——which will be longer than I desire or deserve——Lollo shall want nothing, but——you. I have too little tenderness for——my dear boy, you're faint. Can you spare me for a moment ? "

" No, stay—Major !"

" What ? What ? "

" My head drifts so—if you wouldn't mind."

" Yes ! Yes !"

" Say a prayer by me. Out loud please, I am getting deaf."

" My dearest Jackanapes—my dear boy——"

" One of the Church Prayers—Parade Service, you know——"

" I see.   But the fact is—GOD forgive me, Jackanapes
—I'm a very different sort of fellow to some of you
youngsters.   Look here, let me fetch———"

But Jackanapes' hand was in his, and it wouldn't let go.

There was a brief and bitter silence.

" 'Pon my soul I can only remember the little one at
the end."

" Please," whispered Jackanapes.

Pressed by the conviction that what little he could do it
was his duty to do, the Major—kneeling—bared his head,
and spoke loudly, clearly, and very reverently—

" The Grace of our Lord Jesus Christ———"

Jackanapes moved his left hand to his right one, which
still held the Major's—

" —The love of GOD."

And with that—Jackanapes died.

CHAPTER VI.

"Und so ist der blaue Himmel grösser als jedes
Gewölk darin, und dauerhafter dazu."

JEAN PAUL RICHTER.

ACKANAPES' death was sad news for
the Goose Green, a sorrow just qualified
by honourable pride in his gallantry
and devotion. Only the Cobbler dissented, but
that was his way. He said he saw nothing in it
but foolhardiness and vainglory. They might
both have been killed, as easy as not, and then
where would ye have been? A man's life was a man's life,
and one life was as good as another No one would catch
him throwing his away. And, for that matter, Mrs. Johnson could spare a child a great deal better than Miss
Jessamine.

But the parson preached Jackanapes' funeral sermon
on the text, "Whosoever will save his life shall lose it;
and whosoever will lose his life for My sake shall find it;"
and all the village went and wept to hear him.

Nor did Miss Jessamine see her loss from the Cobbler's
point of view. On the contrary, Mrs. Johnson said she
never to her dying day should forget how, when she went
to condole with her, the old lady came forward, with
gentlewomanly self-control, and kissed her, and thanked
GOD that her dear nephew's effort had been blessed with

success, and that this sad war had made no gap in her friend's large and happy home circle.

"But she's a noble, unselfish woman," sobbed Mrs. Johnson, "and she taught Jackanapes to be the same, and that's how it is that my Tony has been spared to me. And it must be sheer goodness in Miss Jessamine, for what can she know of a mother's feelings? And I'm sure most people seem to think that if you've a large family you don't know one from another any more than they do, and that a lot of children are like a lot of store-apples, if one's taken it won't be missed."

Lollo—the first Lollo, the Gipsy's Lollo—very aged, draws Miss Jessamine's bath-chair slowly up and down the Goose Green in the sunshine.

The Ex-postman walks beside him, which Lollo tolerates to the level of his shoulder. If the Postman advances any nearer to his head, Lollo quickens his pace, and were the Postman to persist in the injudicious attempt,

there is, as Miss Jessamine says, no knowing what might
happen.

In the opinion of the Goose Green, Miss Jessamine has
borne her troubles "wonderfully." Indeed, to-day, some
of the less delicate and less intimate of those who see
everything from the upper windows, say (well behind her
back) that "the old lady seems quite lively with her military beaux again."

The meaning of this is, that Captain Johnson is leaning
over one side of her chair, whilst by the other bends a
brother officer who is staying with him, and who has mani-
fested an extraordinary interest in Lollo. He bends lower
and lower, and Miss Jessamine calls to the Postman to
request Lollo to be kind enough to stop, whilst she is
fumbling for something which always hangs by her side,
and has got entangled with her spectacles.

It is a twopenny trumpet, bought years ago in the village
fair, and over it she and Captain Johnson tell, as best they
can, between them, the story of Jackanapes' ride across the
Goose Green ; and how he won Lollo—the Gipsy's Lollo—
—the racer Lollo—dear Lollo—faithful Lollo—Lollo the
never vanquished—Lollo the tender servant of his old mistress. And Lollo's ears twitch at every mention of his name.

Their hearer does not speak, but he never moves his
eyes from the trumpet, and when the tale is told, he
lifts Miss Jessamine's hand and presses his heavy black
moustache in silence to her trembling fingers.

The sun, setting gently to his rest, embroiders the
sombre foliage of the oak-tree with threads of gold. The
Grey Goose is sensible of an atmosphere of repose, and
puts up one leg for the night. The grass glows with a
more vivid green, and, in answer to a ringing call from
Tony, his sisters, fluttering over the daisies in pale-hued
muslins, come out of their ever-open door, like pretty
pigeons from a dovecote.

And, if the good gossips' eyes do not deceive them, all the Miss Johnsons, and both the officers, go wandering off into the lanes, where bryony wreaths still twine about the brambles.

    *   *   *   *   *   *

A sorrowful story, and ending badly?

Nay, Jackanapes, for the end is not yet.

A life wasted that might have been useful?

Men who have died for men, in all ages, forgive the thought!

There is a heritage of heroic example and noble obligation, not reckoned in the Wealth of Nations, but essential to a nation's life ; the contempt of which, in any people, may, not slowly, mean even its commercial fall.

Very sweet are the uses of prosperity, the harvests of

peace and progress, the fostering sunshine of health and
happiness, and length of days in the land.

But there be things—oh, sons of what has deserved the
name of Great Britain, forget it not!—"the good of" which
and "the use of" which are beyond all calculation of
wordly goods and earthly uses; things such as Love, and
Honour, and the Soul of Man, which cannot be bought
with a price, and which do not die with death. And they
who would fain live happily EVER after, should not leave
these things out of the lessons of their lives.

DADDY DARWIN'S DOVECOT.

DADDY DARWIN'S DOVECOT

A Country Tale by
JULIANA HORATIA EWING
Author of
JACKANAPES &c..

ILLUSTRATED
BY
RANDOLPH
CALDECOTT

PREAMBLE.

A SUMMER'S afternoon. Early in the summer, and late in the afternoon ; with odours and colours deepening, and shadows lengthening, towards evening.

Two gaffers gossiping, seated side by side upon a Yorkshire wall. A wall of sandstone of many colours, glowing redder and yellower as the sun goes down ; well cushioned with moss and lichen, and deep set in rank grass on this side, where the path runs, and in blue hyacinths on that side, where the wood is, and where—on the gray and still naked branches of young oaks—sit divers crows, not less solemn than the gaffers, and also gossiping.

One gaffer in work-day clothes, not unpicturesque of form and hue. Grey, home-knit stockings, and coat and knee-breeches of corduroy, which takes tints from Time and Weather as harmoniously as wooden palings do ; so that field labourers (like some insects) seem to absorb or mimic the colours of the vegetation round them and of their native soil. That is, on work-days. Sunday-best is a different matter, and in this the other gaffer was clothed. He was dressed like the crows above him, *fit excepted:* the reason for which was, that he was only a visitor, a

revisitor to the home of his youth, and wore his Sunday
(and funeral) suit to mark the holiday.

Continuing the path, a stone pack-horse track, leading
past a hedge snow-white with may, and down into a little
wood, from the depths of which one could hear a brook
babbling.   Then up across the sunny field beyond, and yet
up over another field to where the brow of the hill is
crowned by old farm-buildings standing against the sky.

Down this stone path a young man going whistling
home to tea.   Then staying to bend a swarthy face to the
white may to smell it, and then plucking a huge branch on
which the blossom lies like a heavy fall of snow, and throwing that aside for a better, and tearing off another and yet
another, with the prodigal recklessness of a pauper ; and
so, whistling, on into the wood with his arms full.

Down the sunny field, as he goes up it, a woman coming to meet him—with *her* arms full.   Filled by a child
with a may-white frock, and hair shining with the warm
colours of the sandstone.   A young woman, having a fair
forehead visible a long way off, and buxom cheeks, and
steadfast eyes.   When they meet he kisses her, and she
pulls his dark hair and smooths her own, and cuffs him in
country fashion.   Then they change burdens, and she takes
the may into her apron (stooping to pick up fallen bits), and
the child sits on the man's shoulder, and cuffs and lugs its
father as the mother did, and is chidden by her and kissed
by him.   And all the babbling of their chiding and crow-
ing and laughter comes across the babbling of the brook to
the ears of the old gaffers gossiping on the wall.

Gaffer I. spits out an over-munched stalk of meadow
soft-grass, and speaks :

" D'ye see yon chap ? "

Gaffer II. takes up his hat and wipes it round with a
spotted handkerchief (for your Sunday hat is a heating
thing for work-day wear) and puts it on, and makes reply :

"Aye. But he beats me. And—see there!—he's t' first that's beat me yet. Why, lad! I've met young chaps to-day I could ha' sworn to for mates of mine forty years back—if I hadn't ha' been i' t' churchyard spelling over their fathers' tumstuns!"

"Aye. There's a many old standards gone home o' lately."

"What do they call *him*?"

"T'young chap?"

"Aye."

"They *call* him—Darwin."

"Dar—win? I should know a Darwin. They're old standards, is Darwins. What's he to Daddy Darwin of t' Dovecot yonder?"

"He *owns* t' Dovecot. Did ye see t' lass?"

"Aye. Shoo's his missus, I reckon?"

"Aye."

"What did they call her?"

"Phœbe Shaw they called her. And if she'd been *my* lass—but that's nother here nor there, and he's got t' Dovecot."

"Shaw? *They're* old standards, is Shaws. Phœbe? They called her mother Phœbe. Phœbe Johnson. She were a dainty lass! My father were very fond of Phœbe Johnson. He said she allus put him i' mind of our orchard on drying days; pink and white apple-blossom and clean clothes. And yon's her daughter? Where d'ye say t'young chap come from? He don't look like hereabouts."

"He don't come from hereabouts. And yet he do come from hereabouts, as one may say. Look ye here. He come from t' wukhus. That's the short and the long of it."

"*The workhouse?*"

"Aye."

Stupefaction. The crows chattering wildly overhead.

"And he owns Darwin's Dovecot?"

" He owns Darwin's Dovecot."

" And how i' t' name o' all things did that come about ? "

" Why, I'll tell thee.   It was i' this fashion."

*   *   *   *   *   *   *

Not without reason does the wary writer put gossip in the mouths of gaffers rather than of gammers. Male gossips love scandal as dearly as female gossips do, and they bring to it the stronger relish and energies of their sex. But these were country gaffers, whose speech—like shadows—grows lengthy in the leisurely hours of eventide. The gentle reader shall have the tale in plain narration.

NOTE.—It will be plain to the reader that the birds here described are Rooks (*corvus frugilegus*). I have allowed myself to speak of them by their generic or family name of Crow, this being a common country practice. The genus *corvus*, or *Crow*, includes the Raven, the Carrion Crow, the Hooded Crow, the Jackdaw, and the Rook.

SCENE I.

NE Saturday night (some eighteen years earlier than the date of this gaffer-gossiping) the parson's daughter sat in her own room before the open drawer of a bandy-legged black oak table, *balancing her bags.* The bags were money-bags, and the matter shall be made clear at once.

In this parish, as in others, progress and the multiplication of weapons with which civilization and the powers of goodness push their conquests over brutality and the powers of evil, had added to the original duties of the parish priest, a multifarious and all but impracticable variety of offices ; which, in ordinary and laïc conditions, would have been performed by several more or less salaried clerks, bankers, accountants, secretaries, librarians, club-committees, teachers, lecturers, discount for ready-money dealers in clothing, boots, blankets, and coal, domestic-servant agencies, caterers for the public amusement, and preservers of the public peace.

The country parson (no less than statesmen and princes, than men of science and of letters) is responsible for a great deal of his work that is really done by the help-mate

—woman.   This explains why five out of the young lady's·
money-bags bore the following inscriptions in marking-ink :
" Savings' bank," " Clothing club," " Library," " Magazines
and hymn-books," " Three-halfpenny club"—and only three
bore reference to private funds, as—" House-money "—
" Allowance "—" Charity."

It was the bag bearing this last and greatest name
which the parson's daughter now seized and emptied into
her lap.   A ten-shilling piece, some small silver, and twopence halfpenny jingled together, and roused a silver-
haired, tawny-pawed terrier, who left the hearthrug and
came to smell what was the matter.   His mistress's right
hand—absently caressing—quieted his feelings ; and with
the left she held the ten-shilling piece between finger and
thumb, and gazed thoughtfully at the other bags as they
squatted in a helpless row, with twine-tied mouths hanging
on all sides.   It was only after anxious consultation with
an account-book that the half-sovereign was exchanged for
silver ; thanks to the clothing-club bag, which looked
leaner for the accommodation.   In the three-halfpenny
bag (which bulged with pence) some silver was further
solved into copper, and the charity bag was handsomely
distended before the whole lot was consigned once more to
the table-drawer.

Any one accustomed to book-keeping must smile at
this bag-keeping of accounts ; but the parson's daughter
could never " bring her mind " to keeping the funds apart
on paper, and mixing the actual cash.   Indeed, she could
never have brought her conscience to it.   Unless she had
taken the tenth for " charity " from her dress and pocket-
money in coin, and put it then and there into the charity
bag, this self-imposed rule of the duty of almsgiving would
not have been performed to her soul's peace.

The problem which had been exercising her mind that
Saturday night was how to spend what was left of her

benevolent fund in a treat for the children of the neighbouring workhouse. The fund was low, and this had decided the matter. The following Wednesday would be her
twenty-first birthday. If the children came to tea with
her, the foundation of the entertainment would, in the
natural course of things, be laid in the Vicarage kitchen.
The charity bag would provide the extras of the feast.
Nuts, toys, and the like.

When the parson's daughter locked the drawer of the
bandy-legged table, she did so with the vigour of one who
has made up her mind, and set about the rest of her Saturday night's duties without further delay.

She put out her Sunday clothes, and her Bible and
Prayer-book, and class-book and pencil, on the oak chest
at the foot of the bed. She brushed and combed the
silver-haired terrier, who looked abjectly depressed whilst
this was doing, and preposterously proud when it was done.
She washed her own hair, and studied her Sunday-school
lesson for the morrow whilst it was drying. She spread
a coloured quilt at the foot of her white one, for the terrier
to sleep on—a slur which he always deeply resented.

Then she went to bed, and slept as one ought to sleep
on Saturday night, who is bound to be at the Sunday
School by 9.15 on the following morning, with a clear
mind on the Rudiments of the Faith, the history of the
Prophet Elisha, and the destinations of each of the parish
magazines.

SCENE II.

ATHERLESS—mother-less—homeless!

A little workhouse-boy, with a swarthy face and tidily-cropped black hair, as short and thick as the fur of a mole, was grubbing, not quite so cleverly as a mole, in the workhouse garden.

He had been set to weed, but the weeding was very irregularly performed, for his eyes and heart were in the clouds, as he could see them over the big boundary wall. For there—now dark against the white, now white against the gray—some Air Tumbler pigeons were turning summersaults on their homeward way, at such short and regular intervals that they seemed to be tying knots in their lines of flight.

It was too much! The small gardener shamelessly abandoned his duties, and, curving his dirty paws on each

side of his mouth, threw his whole soul into shouting words
of encouragement to the distant birds.

"That's a good un!   On with thee!   Over ye go!
Oo—ooray!"

It was this last prolonged cheer which drowned the
sound of footsteps on the path behind him, so that if he
had been a tumbler pigeon himself he could not have
jumped more nimbly when a man's hand fell upon his
shoulder.   Up went his arms to shield his ears from a
well-merited cuffing; but fate was kinder to him than he
deserved.   It was only an old man (prematurely aged with
drink and consequent poverty), whose faded eyes seemed
to rekindle as he also gazed after the pigeons, and spoke
as one who knows.

"Yon's Daddy Darwin's Tumblers."

"This old pauper had only lately come into "the House"
(the house that never was a home!), and the boy clung
eagerly to his flannel sleeve, and plied him thick and fast
with questions about the world without the workhouse-
walls, and about the happy owner of those yet happier
creatures who were free not only on the earth but in the
skies.

The poor old pauper was quite as willing to talk as the
boy was to listen.   It restored some of that self-respect
which we lose under the consequences of our follies to be
able to say that Daddy Darwin and he had been mates
together, and had had pigeon-fancying in common "many
a long year afore" he came into the House.

And so these two made friendship over such matters as
will bring man and boy together to the end of time.   And
the old pauper waxed eloquent on the feats of Homing
Birds and Tumblers, and on the points of Almonds and
Barbs, Fantails and Pouters; sprinkling his narrative also
with high-sounding and heterogeneous titles, such as
Dragons and Archangels, Blue Owls and Black Priests,

Jacobines, English Horsemen and Trumpeters. And through much boasting of the high stakes he had had on this and that pigeon-match then, and not a few bitter complaints of the harsh hospitality of the House he "had come to " now, it never seemed to occur to him to connect the two, or to warn the lad who hung upon his lips that one cannot eat his cake with the rash appetites of youth, and yet hope to have it for the support and nourishment of his old age.

The longest story the old man told was of a " bit of a trip " he had made to Liverpool, to see some Antwerp Carriers flown from thence to Ghent, and he fixed the date of this by remembering that his twin sons were born in his absence, and that though their birthday was the very day of the race, his " missus turned stoopid," as women (he warned the boy) are apt to do, and refused to have them christened by uncommon names connected with the fancy. All the same, he bet the lads would have been nicknamed the Antwerp Carriers, and known as such to the day of their death, if this had not come so soon and so suddenly, of croup ; when (as it oddly chanced) he was off on another " bit of a holiday " to fly some pigeons of his own in Lincolnshire.

This tale had not come to an end when a voice of authority called for " Jack March," who rubbed his mole-like head and went ruefully off, muttering that he should " catch it now."

" Sure enough ! sure enough !" chuckled the unamiable old pauper.

But again Fate was kinder to the lad than his friend. His negligent weeding passed unnoticed, because he was wanted in a hurry to join the other children in the school-room. The parson's daughter had come, the children were about to sing to her, and Jack's voice could not be dispensed with.

"Sacred Song."

He " cleaned himself" with alacrity, and taking his place in the circle of boys standing with their hands be-hind their backs, he lifted up a voice worthy of a cathedral choir, whilst varying the monotony of sacred song by secretly snatching at the tail of the terrier as it went snuff-ing round the legs of the group. And in this feat he proved as much superior to the rest of the boys (who also tried it) as he excelled them in the art of singing.

Later on he learnt that the young lady had come to invite them all to have tea with her on her birthday. Later still he found the old pauper once more, and ques-tioned him closely about the village and the Vicarage, and as to which of the parishioners kept pigeons, and where.

And when he went to his straw bed that night, and his black head throbbed with visions and high hopes, these were not entirely of the honour of drinking tea with a pretty young lady, and how one should behave himself in such abashing circumstances. He did not even dream principally of the possibility of getting hold of that silver-haired, tawny-pawed dog by the tail under freer conditions than those of this afternoon, though that was a refreshing thought.

What kept him long awake was thinking of this. From the top of an old walnut-tree at the top of a field at the back of the Vicarage, you could see a hill, and on the top of the hill some farm buildings. And it was here (so the old pauper had told him) that those pretty pigeons lived, who, though free to play about among the clouds, yet con-descended to make an earthly home—in Daddy Darwin's Dovecot.

SCENE III.

TWO and two, girls and boys, the young lady's guests marched down to the Vicarage. The schoolmistress was anxious that each should carry his and her tin mug, so as to give as little trouble as possible; but this was resolutely declined, much to the children's satisfaction, who had their walk with free hands, and their tea out of teacups and saucers like anybody else.

It was a fine day, and all went well. The children enjoyed themselves, and behaved admirably into the bargain. There was only one suspicion of misconduct, and the matter was so far from clear that the parson's daughter hushed it up, and, so to speak, dismissed the case.

The children were playing at some game in which Jack March was supposed to excel, but when they came to look for him he could nowhere be found. At last he was discovered, high up among the branches of an old walnut-tree at the top of the field, and though his hands were unstained and his pockets empty, the gardener, who

F

had been the first to spy him, now loudly denounced him as an ungrateful young thief. Jack, with swollen eyes and cheeks besmirched with angry tears, was vehemently declaring that he had only climbed the tree to "have a look at Master Darwin's pigeons," and had not picked so much as a leaf, let alone a walnut; and the gardener, "shaking the truth out of him" by the collar of his fustian jacket, was preaching loudly on the sin of adding falsehood to theft, when the parson's daughter came up, and, in the end, acquitted poor Jack, and gave him leave to amuse himself as he pleased.

It did not please Jack to play with his comrades just then. He felt sulky and aggrieved. He would have liked to play with the terrier who had stood by him in his troubles, and barked at the gardener; but that little friend now trotted after his mistress, who had gone to choir-practice.

Jack wandered about among the shubberies. By-and-by he heard sounds of music, and led by these he came to a gate in a wall, dividing the Vicarage garden from the churchyard. Jack loved music, and the organ and the voices drew him on till he reached the church porch; but there he was startled by a voice that was not only not the voice of song, but was the utterance of a moan so doleful that it seemed the outpouring of all his own lonely, and outcast, and injured feelings in one comprehensive howl.

It was the voice of the silver-haired terrier. He was sitting in the porch, his nose up, his ears down, his eyes shut, his mouth open, bewailing in bitterness of spirit the second and greater crook of his lot.

To what purpose were all the caresses and care and indulgence of his mistress, the daily walks, the weekly washings and combings, the constant companionship, when she betrayed her abiding sense of his inferiority, first, by not letting him sleep on the white quilt, and secondly, by never allowing him to go to church?

Jack shared the terrier's mood. What were tea and plum-cake to him, when his pauper-breeding was so stamped upon him that the gardener was free to say—"A nice tale too! What's thou to do wi' doves, and thou a work'us lad?"—and to take for granted that he would thieve and lie if he got the chance?

His disabilities were not the dog's, however. The parish church was his as well as another's, and he crept inside and leaned against one of the stone pillars, as if it were a big, calm friend.

Far away, under the transept, a group of boys and men held their music near to their faces in the waning light. Among them towered the burly choirmaster, bâton in hand. The parson's daughter was at the organ. Well accustomed to produce his voice to good purpose, the choirmaster's words were clearly to be heard throughout the building, and it was on the subject of articulation and emphasis, and the like, that he was speaking; now and then throwing in an extra aspirate in the energy of that enthusiasm without which teaching is not worth the name.

" That'll not do. We must have it altogether different. You two lads are singing like bumble-bees in a pitcher —horder there, boys!—it's no laughing matter—put down those papers and keep your eyes on me—inflate the chest—" (his own seemed to fill the field of vision) " and try and give forth those noble words as if you'd an idea what they meant."

No satire was intended or taken here, but the two boys, who were practising their duet in an anthem, laid down the music, and turned their eyes on their teacher.

" I'll run through the recitative," he added, "and take your time from the stick. And mind that OH."

The parson's daughter struck a chord, and then the burly choirmaster spoke with the voice of melody :

" My heart is disquieted within me. My heart—my heart is disquieted within me. And the fear of death is fallen—is fallen upon me."

The terrier moaned without, and Jack thought no boy's voice could be worth listening to after that of the choirmaster. But he was wrong. A few more notes from the organ, and then, as night-stillness in a wood is broken by the nightingale, so upon the silence of the church a boy-alto's voice broke forth in obedience to the choirmaster's uplifted hand :

" *Then*, I said—I said——"

Jack gasped, but even as he strained his eyes to see what such a singer could look like, with higher, clearer notes the soprano rose above him—" Then I sa—a—id," and the duet began :

" OH that I had wings—O that I had wings like a dove ! "

Soprano.—" Then would I flee away." *Alto.*—" Then would I flee away." *Together.*—" And be at rest—flee away and be at rest."

The clear young voices soared and chased each other among the arches, as if on the very pinions for which they prayed. Then—swept from their seats by an upward sweep of the choirmaster's arms—the chorus rose, as birds rise, and carried on the strain.

It was not a very fine composition, but this final chorus had the singular charm of fugue. And as the voices mourned like doves, " Oh that I had wings ! " and pursued each other with the plaintive passage, " Then would I flee away—then would I flee away——," Jack's ears knew no weariness of the repetition. It was strangely like watching the rising and falling of Daddy Darwin's pigeons, as they tossed themselves by turns upon their homeward flight.

After the fashion of the piece and period, the chorus was repeated, and the singers rose to supreme effort. The choirmaster's hands flashed hither and thither, controlling, inspiring, directing. He sang among the tenors.

Jack's voice nearly choked him with longing to sing too. Could words of man go more deeply home to a young heart caged within workhouse walls?

"Oh that I had wings like a dove! Then would I flee away—" the choirmaster's white hands were fluttering downwards in the dusk, and the chorus sank with them— "flee away and be at rest!"

SCENE IV.

ACK MARCH had a busy little brain, and his nature was not of the limp type that sits down with a grief. That most memorable tea-party had fired his soul with two distinct ambitions. First, to be a choir-boy; and, secondly, to dwell in Daddy Darwin's Dovecot. He turned the matter over in his mind, and patched together the following facts:

The Board of Guardians meant to apprentice him, Jack, to some master, at the earliest opportunity. Daddy Darwin (so the old pauper told him) was a strange old man, who had come down in the world, and now lived quite alone, with not a soul to help him in the house or outside it. He was "not to say *mazelin* yet, but getting helpless, and uncommon mean."

A nephew came one fine day and fetched away the old pauper, to his great delight. It was by their hands that Jack despatched a letter, which the nephew stamped and posted for him, and which was duly delivered on the following morning to Mr. Darwin of the Dovecot.

The old man had no correspondents, and he looked

"Daddy Darwin faces the Board."

long at the letter before he opened it.   It did credit to the
teaching of the workhouse schoolmistress :

" HONOURED SIR,

  "They call me Jack March.   I'm a workhouse lad, but. Sir, I'm
a good one, and the Board means to 'prentice me next time.   Sir, if you face
the Board and take me out you shall never regret it.   Though I says it as
shouldn't I'm a handy lad.   I'll clean a floor with any one, and am willing to
work early and late, and at your time of life you're not what you was, and
them birds must take a deal of seeing to.   I can see them from the garden
when I'm set to weed, and I never saw nought like them.   Oh, Sir, I do beg
and pray you let me mind your pigeons.   You'll be none the worse of a lad
about the place, and I shall be happy all the days of my life.   Sir, I'm not
unthankful, but, please GOD, I should like to have a home, and to be with
them house doves.

           " From your humble servant—hoping to be—

                               "JACK MARCH.

  " Mr. Darwin, Sir.   I love them Tumblers as if they was my own."

Daddy Darwin thought hard and thought long over
that letter. He changed his mind fifty times a day. But
Friday was the Board day, and when Friday came he
" faced the Board."   And the little workhouse lad went
home to Daddy Darwin's Dovecot.

SCENE V.

HE bargain was oddly made, but it worked well. Whatever Jack's parentage may have been (and he was named after the stormy month in which he had been born), the blood that ran in his veins could not have been beggars' blood. There was no hopeless, shiftless, invincible idleness about him. He found work for himself when it was not given him to do, and he attached himself passionately and proudly to all the belongings of his new home.

"Yon lad of yours seem handy enough, Daddy ;—for a vagrant, as one may say."

Daddy Darwin was smoking over his garden wall, and Mrs. Shaw, from the neighbouring farm, had paused in her walk for a chat. She was a notable housewife, and there was just a touch of envy in her sense of the improved appearance of the doorsteps and other visible points of the Dovecot. Daddy Darwin took his pipe out of his mouth to make way for the force of his reply :

"*Vagrant !* Nay, missus, yon's no vagrant. *He's fettling up all along.* Jack's the sort that if he finds a key he'll look for the lock ; if ye give him a knife-blade

he'll fashion a heft.   Why, a vagrant's a chap that, if he'd
all your maester owns to-morrow, he'd be on the tramp
again afore t' year were out, and three years wouldn't
repair the mischief he'd leave behind him.   A vagrant's a
chap that if ye lend him a thing he loses it ; if ye give him
a thing he abuses it——"

"That's true enough, and there's plenty servant-girls
the same," put in Mrs. Shaw.

"Maybe there be, ma'am—maybe there be ; vagrants'
children, I reckon.   But yon little chap I got from t' House
comes of folk that's had stuff o' their own, and cared for it
—choose who they were."

"Well, Daddy," said his neighbour, not without malice,
"I'll wish you a good evening.   You've got a good bargain
out of the parish, it seems."

But Daddy Darwin only chuckled, and stirred up the
ashes in the bowl of his pipe.

"The same to you, ma'am—the same to you.   Aye!
he's a good bargain—a very good bargain is Jack March."

It might be supposed from the foregoing dialogue that
Daddy Darwin was a model householder, and the little
workhouse boy the neatest creature breathing.   But the
gentle reader who may imagine this is much mistaken.

Daddy Darwin's Dovecot was freehold, and when he
inherited it from his father there was still attached to it
a good bit of the land that had passed from father to son
through more generations than the church registers were
old enough to record.   But the few remaining acres were so
heavily mortgaged that they had to be sold.   So that a bit
of house property elsewhere, and the old homestead itself,
were all that was left.   And Daddy Darwin had never been
the sort of man to retrieve his luck at home, or to seek it
abroad.

That he had inherited a somewhat higher and more
refined nature than his neighbours had rather hindered than

helped him to prosper.   And he had been unlucky in love.
When what energies he had were in their prime, his father's
death left him with such poor prospects that the old farmer
to whose daughter he was betrothed broke off the match
and married her elsewhere.   His Alice was not long another
man's wife.   She died within a year from her wedding-day,
and her husband married again within a year from her
death.   Her old lover was no better able to mend his
broken heart than his broken fortunes.   He only banished
women from the Dovecot, and shut himself up from the
coarse consolation of his neighbours.

In this loneliness, eating a kindly heart out in bitterness
of spirit, with all that he ought to have had—

> To plough and sow
> And reap and mow—

gone from him, and in the hands of strangers ; the pigeons,
for which the Dovecot had always been famous, became
the business and the pleasure of his life.   But of late years
his stock had dwindled, and he rarely went to pigeon-
matches or competed in shows and races.   A more miserable fancy rivalled his interest in pigeon fancying.   His new
hobby was hoarding ; and money that, a few years back, he
would have freely spent to improve his breed of Tumblers
or back his Homing Birds he now added with stealthy
pleasure to the store behind the secret panel of a fine old
oak bedstead that had belonged to the Darwyn who owned
Dovecot when the sixteenth century was at its latter end.
In this bedstead Daddy slept lightly of late, as old men
will, and he had horrid dreams, which old men need not
have.   The queer faces carved on the panels (one of which
hid the money hole) used to frighten him when he was a
child.   They did not frighten him now by their grotesque
ugliness, but when he looked at them, *and knew which was
which*, he dreaded the dying out of twilight into dark, and

dreamed of aged men living alone, who had been murdered for their savings. These growing fears had had no small share in deciding him to try Jack March ; and to see the lad growing stronger, nimbler, and more devoted to his master's interests day by day, was a nightly comfort to the poor old hoarder in the bed-head.

As to his keen sense of Jack's industry and carefulness, it was part of the incompleteness of Daddy Darwin's nature, and the ill-luck of his career, that he had a sensitive perception of order and beauty, and a shrewd observation of ways of living and qualities of character, and yet had allowed his early troubles to blight him so completely that he never put forth an effort to rise above the ruin, of which he was at least as conscious as his neighbours.

That Jack was not the neatest creature breathing, one look at him, as he stood with pigeons on his head and arms and shoulders, would have been enough to prove. As the first and readiest repudiation of his workhouse antecedents he had let his hair grow till it hung in the wildest elf-locks, and though the terms of his service with Daddy Darwin would not, in any case, have provided him with handsome clothes, such as he had were certainly not the better for any attention he bestowed upon them. As regarded the Dovecot, however, Daddy Darwin had not done more than justice to his bargain. A strong and grateful attachment to his master, and a passionate love for the pigeons he tended, kept Jack constantly busy in the service of both ; the old pigeon-fancier taught him the benefits of scrupulous cleaniness in the pigeon-cote, and Jack "stoned" the kitchen-floor and the doorsteps on his own responsibility.

The time did come when he tidied up himself.

SCENE VI.

ADDY DARWIN had made the first breach in his solitary life of his own free will, but it was fated to widen. The parson's daughter soon heard that he had got a lad from the workhouse, the very boy who sang so well and had climbed the walnut-tree to look at Daddy Darwin's pigeons. The most obvious parish questions at once presented themselves to the young lady's mind. "Had the boy been christened? Did he go to Church and Sunday-school? Did he say his prayers and know his Catechism? Had he a Sunday suit? Would he do for the choir?"

Then, supposing (a not uncommon case) that the boy *had* been christened, *said* he said his prayers, *knew* his Catechism, and *was* ready for school, church, and choir, but had not got a Sunday suit—a fresh series of riddles

propounded themselves to her busy brain. "Would her
father yield up his every-day coat and take his Sunday
one into week-day wear? Could the charity bag do better
than pay the tailor's widow for adapting this old coat to
the new chorister's back, taking it in at the seams, turning
it wrong-side out, and getting new sleeves out of the old
tails? Could she herself spare the boots which the village
cobbler had just resoled for her—somewhat clumsily—and
would the "allowance" bag bear this strain? Might she
hope to coax an old pair of trowsers out of her cousin, who
was spending his Long Vacation at the Vicarage, and who
never reckoned very closely with *his* allowance, and kept
no charity bag at all? Lastly would "that old curmudgeon
at the Dovecot" let his little farm-boy go to church and
school and choir?

"I must go and persuade him," said the young lady.

What she said, and what (at the time) Daddy Darwin
said, Jack never knew. He was at high sport with the
terrier round the big sweet-brier bush, when he saw his old
master slitting the seams of his weather-beaten coat in
the haste with which he plucked crimson clove carnations
as if they had been dandelions, and presented them, not
ungracefully, to the parson's daughter.

Jack knew why she had come, and strained his ears to
catch his own name. But Daddy Darwin was promising
pipings of the cloves.

"They are such dear old-fashioned things," said she,
burying her nose in the bunch.

"We're old-fashioned altogether, here, Miss," said Daddy
Darwin, looking wistfully at the tumble-down house behind
them.

"You're very pretty here," said she, looking also, and
thinking what a sketch it would make, if she could keep on
friendly terms with this old recluse, and get leave to sit in
the garden. Then her conscience smiting her for selfish-

ness, she turned her big eyes on him and put out her small hand.

"I am very much obliged to you, Mr. Darwin, very much obliged to you indeed. And I hope that Jack will do credit to your kindness. And thank you so much for the cloves," she added, hastily changing a subject which had cost some argument, and which she did not wish to have reopened.

Daddy Darwin had thoughts of reopening it. He was slowly getting his ideas together to say that the lad should see how he got along with the school before trying the choir, when he found the young lady's hand in his, and had to take care not to hurt it, whilst she rained thanks on him for the flowers.

"You're freely welcome, Miss," was what he did say after all.

In the evening, however, he was very moody, but Jack was dying of curiosity, and at last could contain himself no longer.

"What did Miss Jenny want, Daddy?" he asked.

The old man looked very grim.

"First to mak a fool of me, and i' t' second place to mak a fool of thee," was his reply. And he added with pettish emphasis, "They're all alike, gentle and simple. Lad, lad! If ye'd have any peace of your life never let a woman's foot across your threshold. Steek t' door of your house— if ye own one—and t' door o' your heart—if ye own one— and then ye'll never rue. Look at this coat!"

And the old man went grumpily to bed, and dreamed that Miss Jenny had put her little foot over his threshold, and that he had shown her the secret panel, and let her take away his savings.

And Jack went to bed, and dreamed that he went to school, and showed himself to Phœbe Shaw in his Sunday suit.

This dainty little damsel had long been making havoc in Jack's heart. The attraction must have been one of contrast, for whereas Jack was black and grubby, and had only week-day clothes—which were ragged at that—Phœbe was fair, and exquisitely clean, and quite terribly tidy. Her mother was the neatest woman in the parish. It was she who was wont to say to her trembling handmaid, "I hope I can black a grate without blacking myself." But little Phœbe promised so far to out-do her mother, that it seemed doubtful if she could "black herself" if she tried. Only the bloom of childhood could have resisted the polishing effects of yellow soap, as Phœbe's brow and cheeks did resist it. Her shining hair was compressed into a plait that would have done credit to a rope-maker. Her pinafores were speckless, and as to her white Whitsun frock—Jack could think of nothing the least like Phœbe in that, except a snowy fantail strutting about the dovecot roof; and, to say the truth, the likeness was most remarkable.

It has been shown that Jack March had a mind to be master of his fate, and he did succeed in making friends with little Phœbe Shaw. This was before Miss Jenny's visit, but the incident shall be recorded here.

Early on Sunday mornings it was Jack's custom to hide his work-day garb in an angle of the ivy-covered wall of the Dovecot garden, only letting his head appear over the top, from whence he watched to see Phœbe pass on her way to Sunday school, and to bewilder himself with the sight of her starched frock, and her airs with her Bible and Prayer-book, and class card, and clean pocket-handkerchief.

Now, amongst the rest of her Sunday paraphernalia, Phœbe always carried a posy, made up with herbs and some strong-smelling flowers. Countrywomen take mint and southernwood to a long hot service, as fine ladies take smelling-bottles (for it is a pleasant delusion with some writers that the weaker sex is a strong sex in the working

classes). And though Phœbe did not suffer from "fainty
feels" like her mother, she and her little playmates took
posies to Sunday school, and refreshed their nerves in the
stream of question and answer, and hair oil and corduroy,
with all the airs of their elders.

One day she lost her posy on her way to school, and
her loss was Jack's opportunity. He had been waiting
half-an-hour among the ivy, when he saw her just below
him, fuzzling round and round like a kitten chasing its tail.
He sprang to the top of the wall.

"Have ye lost something?" he gasped.

"My posy," said poor Phœbe, lifting her sweet eyes,
which were full of tears.

A second spring brought Jack into the dust at her feet,
where he searched most faithfully, and was wandering
along the path by which she had come, when she called
him back.

"Never mind," she said. "They'll most likely be dusty
by now."

Jack was not used to think the worse of anything for a
coating of dust; but he paused, trying to solve the perpetual problem of his situation, and find out what the little
maid really wanted.

"'Twas only Old Man and marygolds," said she.
"They're common enough."

A light illumined Jack's understanding.

"We've Old Man i' plenty. Wait, and I'll get thee a
fresh posy." And he began to reclimb the wall.

But Phœbe drew nearer. She stroked down her frock,
and spoke mincingly but confidentially. "My mother
says Daddy Darwin has red bergamot i' his garden.
We've none i' ours. My mother always says there's
nothing like red bergamot to take to church. She says
it's a deal more refreshing than Old Man, and not so common. My mother says she's always meaning to ask Daddy

G

"*There's* red bergamot; smell it!"

Darwin to let us have a root to set ; but she doesn't often see him, and when she does she doesn't think on. But she always says there's nothing like red bergamot, and my Aunt Nancy, she says the same."

"*Red* is it ?" cried Jack. "You wait there, love." And before Phœbe could say him nay, he was over the wall and back again with his arms full.

"Is it any o' this lot ?" he inquired, dropping a small haycock of flowers at her feet.

" Don't ye know one from t'other ? " asked Phœbe, with round eyes of reproach. And spreading her clean kerchief on the grass she laid her Bible and Prayer-book and class card on it, and set vigorously and nattily to work, picking one flower and another from the fragrant confusion, nipping the stalks to even lengths, rejecting withered leaves, and instructing Jack as she proceeded.

" I suppose ye know a rose ? That's a double velvet.* They dry sweeter than lavender for linen. These dark red things is pheasants' eyes ; but, dear, dear, what a lad ! ye've dragged it up by the roots ! And eh ! what will Master Darwin say when he misses these pink hollyhocks ? And only in bud, too ! *There's* red begamot ;† smell it !"

It had barely touched Jack's willing nose when it was hastily withdrawn. Phœbe had caught sight of Polly and Susan Smith coming to school, and crying that she should be late and must run, the little maid picked up her paraphernalia (not forgetting the red bergamot), and fled down the lane. And Jack, with equal haste, snatched up the tell-tale heap of flowers and threw them into a disused pigsty, where it was unlikely that Daddy Darwin would go to look for his poor pink hollyhocks.

---

* Double velvet, an old summer rose, not common now. It is described by Parkinson.

† Red Bergamot, or Twinflower : *Monarda Didyma.*

SCENE VII.

PRIL was a busy month in the Dovecot. Young birds were chipping the egg, parent birds were feeding their young or relieving each other on the nest, and Jack and his master were constantly occupied and excited.

One night Daddy Darwin went to bed; but, though he was tired, he did not sleep long. He had sold a couple of handsome but quarrelsome pigeons to advantage, and had added their price to the hoard in the bed-head. This had renewed his old fears, for the store was becoming very valuable; and he wondered if it had really escaped Jack's quick observation, or whether the boy knew about it, and, perhaps, talked about it. As he lay and worried himself he fancied he heard sounds without—the sound of footsteps and of voices. Then his heart beat till he could hear nothing else; then he could undoubtedly hear nothing at all; then he certainly heard something which probably was rats. And so he lay in a cold sweat, and pulled the rug over his face, and made up his mind to give the money to the parson, for the poor, if he was spared till daylight.

He *was* spared till daylight, and had recovered himself,

and settled to leave the money where it was, when Jack
rushed in from the pigeon-house with a face of dire dismay.
He made one or two futile efforts to speak, and then un-
consciously used the words Shakespeare has put into the
mouth of Macduff, " All my pretty 'uns !" and so burst into
tears.

And when the old man made his way to the pigeon-
house, followed by poor Jack, he found that the eggs were
cold and the callow young shivering in deserted nests, and
that every bird was gone. And then he remembered the
robbers, and was maddened by the thought that whilst he
lay expecting thieves to break in and steal his money he
had let them get safely off with his whole stock of pigeons.

Daddy Darwin had never taken up arms against his
troubles, and this one crushed him. The fame and beauty
of his house-doves were all that was left of prosperity
about the place, ànd now there was nothing left—*nothing !*
Below this dreary thought lay a far more bitter one, which he
dared not confide to Jack. He had heard the robbers ; he
might have frightened them away ; he might at least have
given the lad a chance to save his pets, and not a care had
crossed his mind except for the safety of his own old bones,
and of those miserable savings in the bedhead, which he
was enduring so much to scrape together (oh satire !) for a
distant connexion whom he had never seen. He crept back
to the kitchen, and dropped in a heap upon the settle, and
muttered to himself. Then his thoughts wandered. Supposing the pigeons were gone for good, would he ever make
up his mind to take that money out of the money-hole, and
buy a fresh stock ? He knew he never would, and shrank
into a meaner heap upon the settle as he said so to himself.
He did not like to look his faithful lad in the face.

Jack looked him in the face, and, finding no help there
acted pretty promptly behind his back. He roused the
parish constable, and fetched that functionary to the Dove-

cot before he had had bite or sup to break his fast. He
spread a meal for him and Daddy, and borrowed the
Shaws' light cart whilst they were eating it. The Shaws
were good farmer-folk, they sympathised most fully; and
Jack was glad of a few words of pity from Phœbe. She
said she had watched the pretty pets "many a score of
times," which comforted more than one of Jack's heart-
strings. Phœbe's mother paid respect to his sense and
promtitude. He had acted exactly as she would have
done.

"Daddy was right enough about yon lad," she admitted.
"He's not one to let the grass grow under his feet."

And she gave him a good breakfast whilst the horse
was being "put to." It pleased her that Jack jumped up
and left half a delicious cold tea-cake behind him when the
cart-wheels grated outside. Mrs. Shaw sent Phœbe to put
the cake in his pocket, and "the Measter" helped Jack
in and took the reins. He said he would "see Daddy
Darwin through it," and added the weight of his opinion to
that of the constable, that the pigeons had been taken to
"a beastly low place" (as he put it) that had lately been
set up for pigeon-shooting in the outskirts of the neighbouring town.

They paused no longer at the Dovecot than was needed
to hustle Daddy Darwin on to the seat beside Master Shaw,
and for Jack to fill his pockets with peas, and take his place
beside the constable. He had certain ideas of his own on
the matter, which were not confused by the jog-trot of the
light cart, which did give a final jumble to poor Daddy
Darwin's faculties.

No wonder they were jumbled! The terrors of the
night past, the shock of the morning, the completeness of
the loss, the piteous sight in the pigeon house, remorseful
shame, and then—after all these years, during which he had
not gone half a mile from his own hearthstone—to be set

up for all the world to see, on the front seat of a market-cart, back to back with the parish constable, and jogged off as if miles were nothing, and crowded streets were nothing, and the Beaulieu Gardens were nothing; Master Shaw talking away as easily as if they were sitting in two arm-chairs, and making no more of " stepping into " a lawyer's office, and " going on " to the Town Hall, than if he were talking of stepping up to his own bedchamber or going out into the garden!

That day passed like a dream, and Daddy Darwin remembered what happened in it as one remembers visions of the night.

He had a vision (a very unpleasing vision) of the proprietor of the Beaulieu Gardens, a big greasy man, with sinister eyes very close together, and a hook nose, and a heavy watchchain, and a bullying voice. He browbeat the constable very soon, and even bullied Master Shaw into silence. No help was to be had from him in his loud indignation at being supposed to traffic with thieves. When he turned the tables by talking of slander, loss of time, and compensation, Daddy Darwin smelt money, and tremblingly whispered to Master Shaw to apologise and get out of it. "They're gone for good," he almost sobbed; "Gone for good, like all t' rest! And I'll not be long after 'em."

But even as he spoke he heard a sound which made him lift up his head. It was Jack's call at feeding-time to the pigeons at the Dovecot. And quick following on this most musical and most familiar sound there came another. The old man put both his lean hands behind his ears to be sure that he heard it aright—the sound of wings—the wings of a dove!

The other men heard it and ran in. Whilst they were wrangling, Jack had slipped past them, and had made his way into a wired enclosure in front of the pigeon-house. And there they found him, with all the captive pigeons coming to his call ; flying, fluttering, strutting, nestling from head to foot of him, he scattering peas like hail.

He was the first to speak, and not a choke in his voice. His iron temperament was at white heat, and, as he afterwards said, he "cared no more for yon dirty chap wi' the big nose, nor if he were a *ratten** in a hayloft !"

"These is ours," he said, shortly. "I'll count 'em over, and see if they're right. There was only one young 'un that could fly. A white 'un." ("It's here," interpolated Master Shaw.) "I'll pack 'em i' yon," and Jack turned his thumb to a heap of hampers in a corner. "T' carrier can leave t' baskets at t' toll-bar next Saturday, and ye may send your lad for 'em, if ye keep one."

The proprietor of the Beaulieu Gardens was not a man easily abashed, but most of the pigeons were packed before he had fairly resumed his previous powers of speech. Then, as Master Shaw said, he talked "on the other side of his mouth." Most willing was he to help to bring to justice the scoundrels who had deceived him and robbed Mr. Darwin, but he feared they would be difficult to trace. His own feeling was that of wishing for pleasantness among neighbours. The pigeons had been found at the Gardens. That was enough. He would be glad to settle the business out of court.

Daddy Darwin heard the chink of the dirty man's money, and would have compounded the matter then and there. But not so the parish constable, who saw himself famous ; and not so Jack, who turned eyes of smouldering fire on Master Shaw.

"Maester Shaw! you'll not let them chaps get off? Daddy's mazelin wi' trouble, sir, but I reckon you'll see to it."

"If it costs t' worth of the pigeons ten times over, I'll see to it, my lad," was Master Shaw's reply. And the

* *Anglicé* Rat.

parish constable rose even to a vein of satire as he avenged himself of the man who had slighted his office. "Settle it out of court? Aye! I dare say. And send t' same chaps to fetch 'em away again t' night after. Nay—bear a hand with this hamper, Maester Shaw, if you please—if it's all t' same to you, Mr. Proprietor, I think we shall have to trouble you to step up to t' Town Hall by-and-by, and see if we can't get shut of them mistaking friends o' yours for three months any way."

If that day was a trying one to Daddy Darwin, the night that followed it was far worse. The thieves were known to the police, and the case was down to come on at the Town Hall the following morning; but meanwhile the constable thought fit to keep the pigeons under his own charge in the village lock-up. Jack refused to be parted from his birds, and remained with them, leaving Daddy Darwin alone in the Dovecot. He dared not go to bed, and it was not a pleasant night that he spent, dozing with weariness, and starting up with fright, in an arm-chair facing the money-hole.

Some things that he had been nervous about he got quite used to, however. He bore himself with sufficient dignity in the publicity of the Town Hall, where a great sensation was created by the pigeons being let loose without, and coming to Jack's call. Some of them fed from the boy's lips, and he was the hero of the hour, to Daddy Darwin's delight.

Then the lawyer and the lawyer's office proved genial and comfortable to him. He liked civil ways and smooth speech, and understood them far better than Master Shaw's brevity and uncouthness. The lawyer chatted kindly and intelligently; he gave Daddy Darwin wine and biscuit, and talked of the long standing of the Darwin family and its vicissitudes; he even took down some fat yellow books, and showed the old man how many curious laws had been

made from time to time for the special protection of
pigeons in Dovecots, very ancient statutes making the
killing of a house-dove felony. Then 1 James I. c. 29
awarded three months' imprisonment "without bail or
mainprice" to any person who should "shoot at, kill, or
destroy with any gun, crossbow, stonebow, or longbow, any
house-dove or pigeon;" but allowed an alternative fine of
twenty shillings to be paid to the churchwardens of the
parish for the benefit of the poor. Daddy Darwin hoped
there was no such alternative in this case, and it proved
that by 2 Geo. III. c. 29, the twenty-shilling fine was trans-
ferred to the owner of birds ; at which point another client
called, and the polite lawyer left Daddy to study the laws
by himself.

It was when Jack was helping Master Shaw to put the
horse into the cart, after the trial was over, that the farmer
said to him, "I don't want to put you about, my lad, but
I'm afraid you won't keep your master long. T'old gentleman's breaking up, mark my words ! Constable and me
was going into the *George* for a glass, and Master Darwin
left us and went back to the office. I says, 'What are ye
going back to t' lawyer for ?' and he says, 'I don't mind
telling you, Master Shaw, but it's to make my will.' And
off he goes. Now, there's only two more things between
that and death, Jack March ! And one's the parson, and
t' other's the doctor."

SCENE VIII.

ITTLE Phœbe Shaw coming out of the day-school, and picking her way home to tea, was startled by folk running past her, and by a sound of cheering from the far end of the village, which gradually increased in volume, and was caught up by the bystanders as they ran. When Phœbe heard that it was "Constable, and Master Shaw, and Daddy Darwin and his lad, coming home, and the pigeons along wi' 'em," she felt inclined to run too ; but a fit of shyness came over her, and she demurely decided to wait by the school-gate till they came her way. They did not come. They stopped. What were they doing? Another by-stander explained, "They're shaking hands wi' Daddy, and I reckon they're making him put up t' birds here, to see 'em go home to t' Dovecot."

Phœbe ran as if for her life. She loved beast and bird as well as Jack himself, and the fame of Daddy Darwin's doves was great. To see them put up by him to fly home after such an adventure was a sight not lightly to be for-gone. The crowd had moved to a hillock in a neighbour-

" Constable, and Master Shaw, and Daddy Darwin, and his lad, coming
home, and the pigeons along wi' 'em."

ing field before she touched its outskirts. By that time it pretty well numbered the population of the village, from the oldest inhabitant to the youngest that could run. Phœbe had her mother's courage and resource. Chirping out feebly but clearly, "I'm Maester Shaw's little lass, will ye let me through?" she was passed from hand to hand, till her little fingers found themselves in Jack's tight clasp, and he fairly lifted her to her father's side.

She was just in time. Some of the birds had hung about Jack, nervous, or expecting peas; but the hesitation was past. Free in the sweet sunshine—beating down the evening air with silver wings and their feathers like gold—ignorant of cold eggs and callow young dead in deserted nests—sped on their way by such a roar as rarely shook the village in its body corporate—they flew straight home:

— to Daddy Darwin's Dovecot.

SCENE IX.

ADDY DAR-
WIN lived
a good
many years
after mak-
ing his will,
and the
Dovecot
prospered
in his hands.
It would
be more
just to
say that
it pros-
pered in
the hands
of Jack
March.

By hook and by crook he increased the live stock about
the place. Folk were kind to one who had set so excellent an example to other farm lads, though he lacked the
primal virtue of belonging to the neighbourhood. He
bartered pigeons for fowls, and some one gave him a sitting of eggs to "see what he would make of 'em." Master
Shaw gave him a little pig, with kind words and good

counsel; and Jack cleaned out the disused pigstyes, which
were never disused again.   He scrubbed his pigs with soap
and water as if they had been Christians, and the admirable
animals, regardless of the pork they were coming to, did
him infinite credit, and brought him profit into the bargain,
which he spent on ducks' eggs, and other additions to his
farmyard family.

The Shaws were very kind to him ; and if Mrs. Shaw's
secrets must be told, it was because Phœbe was so un-
changeably and increasingly kind to him, that she sent the
pretty maid (who had a knack of knowing her own mind
about things) to service.

Jack March was a handsome, stalwart youth now, of
irreproachable conduct, and with qualities which Mrs. Shaw
particularly prized ; but he was but a farm-lad, and no
match for her daughter.

Jack only saw his sweetheart once during several years.
She had not been well, and was at home for the benefit of
"native air."   He walked over the hill with her as they
returned from church, and lived on the remembrance of
that walk for two or three years more.   Phœbe had given
him her Prayer-book to carry, and he had found a dead
flower in it, and had been jealous.   She had asked if he
knew what it was, and he had replied fiercely that he did
not, and was not sure that he cared to know.

"Ye never did know much about flowers," said Phœbe,
demurely, "It's red bergamot."

"I love—red bergamot," he whispered penitently.   "And
thou owes me a bit.   I gave thee some once."   And Phœbe
had let him put the withered bits into his own hymn-book,
which was more than he deserved.

Jack was still in the choir, and taught in the Sunday
school where he used to learn.   The parson's daughter had
had her way ; Daddy Darwin grumbled at first, but in the
end he got a bottle-green Sunday-coat out of the oak-

press that matched the bedstead, and put the house-key
into his pocket, and went to church too. Now, for years
past he had not failed to take his place, week by week, in
the pew that was traditionally appropriated to the use of
the Darwins of Dovecot. In such an hour the sordid cares
of the secret panel weighed less heavily on his soul, and

the things that are not seen came nearer—the house not
made with hands, the treasures that rust and moth corrupt
not, and which thieves do not break through to steal.

Daddy Darwin died of old age. As his health failed,
Jack nursed him with the tenderness of a woman ; and kind

inquiries, and dainties which Jack could not have cooked, came in from many quarters where it pleased the old man to find that he was held in respect and remembrance.

One afternoon, coming in from the farmyard, Jack found him sitting by the kitchen-table as he had left him, but with a dread look of change upon his face. At first he feared there had been "a stroke," but Daddy Darwin's mind was clear and his voice firmer than usual.

"My lad," he said, "fetch me yon tea-pot out of the corner cupboard. T' one wi' a pole-house* painted on it, and some letters. Take care how ye shift it. It were t' merry feast-pot† at my christening, and yon's t' letters of my father's and mother's names. Take off t' lid. There's two bits of paper in the inside."

Jack did as he was bid, and laid the papers (one small and yellow with age, the other bigger, and blue, and neatly written upon) at his master's right hand.

"Read yon," said the old man, pushing the small one towards him. Jack took it up wondering. It was the letter he had written from the workhouse fifteen years before. That was all he could see. The past surged up too thickly before his eyes, and tossing it impetuously from him, he dropped on a chair by the table, and snatching Daddy Darwin's hands he held them to his face with tears.

"GOD bless thee!" he sobbed. "You've been a good maester to me!"

"*Daddy*," wheezed the old man. "*Daddy*, not maester." And drawing his right hand away, he laid it solemnly on the young man's head. "GOD bless *thee*, and reward thee. What have I done i' my feckless life to deserve a son? But if ever a lad earned a father and a home, thou hast earned 'em, Jack March."

---

* A *pole-house* is a small dovecot on the top of a pole.
† "Merry feast-pot" is a name given to old pieces of ware, made in local potteries for local festivals.

H

He moved his hand again and laid it trembling on the paper.

"Every word i' this letter ye've made good. Every word, even to t' bit at the end. 'I love them tumblers as if they were my own,' says you. Lift thee head, lad, and look at me. *They are thy own!* . . . Yon blue paper's my last will and testament, made many a year back by Mr. Brown, of Green Street, Solicitor, and a very nice gentleman too ; and witnessed by his clerks, two decent young chaps, and civil enough, but with too much watchchain for their situation. Jack March, my son, I have left thee maester of Dovecot and all that I have. And there's a bit of money in t' bedhead that 'll help thee to make a fair start, and to bury me decently atop of my father and mother. Ye may let Bill Sexton toll an hour-bell for me, for I'm a old standard, if I never were good for much. Maybe I might ha' done better if things had happed in a different fashion ; but the Lord knows all. I'd like a hymn at the grave, Jack, if the Vicar has no objections, and do thou sing if thee can. Don't fret, my son, thou'st no cause. 'Twas that sweet voice o' thine took me back again to public worship, and it's not t' least of all I owe thee, Jack March. A poor reason lad, for taking up with a neglected duty—a poor reason—but the Lord is a GOD of mercy, or there'd be small chance for most on us. If Miss Jenny and her husband come to t' Vicarage this summer, say I left her my duty and an old man's blessing ; and if she wants any roots out of t' garden, give 'em her, and give her yon old chest that stands in the back chamber. It belonged to an uncle of my mother's—a Derbyshire man. They say her husband's a rich gentleman, and treats her very well. I reckon she may have what she's a mind, new and polished, but she's always for old lumber. They're a whimsical lot, gentle and simple. And talking of *women*, Jack, I've a word to say, if I can fetch my breath to say it.

Lad! as sure as you're maester of Dovecot, you'll give it a
missus.   Now take heed to me.   If ye fetch any woman
home here but Phœbe Shaw, I'll *walk*, and scare ye away
from t' old place.   I'm willing for Phœbe, and I charge ye
to tell the lass so hereafter.   And tell her it's not because
she's fair—too many on 'em are that; and not because
she's thrifty and houseproud—her mother's that, and she's
no favourite of mine; but because I've watched her when-
ever t' ould cat 'o let her be at home, and it's my belief
that she loves ye, knowing nought of *this*" (he laid his
hand upon the will) "and that she'll stick to ye, choose
what her folk may say.   Aye, aye, she's not one of t' sort
that quits a falling house—*like rattens*."

Language fails to convey the bitterness which the old
man put into these last two words.   It exhausted him,
and his mind wandered.   When he had to some extent
recovered himself he spoke again, but very feebly.

"Tak' my duty to the Vicar, lad, Daddy Darwin's duty,
and say he's at t' last feather of the shuttle, and would be
thankful for the Sacrament."

     *   *   *   *   *   *   *

The Parson had come and gone.   Daddy Darwin did
not care to lie down, he breathed with difficulty; so Jack
made him easy in a big arm-chair, and raked up the fire
with cinders, and took a chair on the other side of the
hearth to watch with him.   The old man slept comfortably,
and at last, much wearied, the young man dozed also.

He awoke because Daddy Darwin moved, but for a
moment he thought he must be dreaming.   So erect the
old man stood, and with such delight in his wide-open
eyes.   They were looking over Jack's head.

All that the lad had never seen upon his face seemed to
have come back to it—youth, hope, resolution, tenderness.
His lips were trembling with the smile of acutest joy.

Suddenly he stretched out his arms, and crying, "Alice!" started forward and fell—dead—on the breast of his adopted son.

RAW! Craw! Craw! The crows flapped slowly home, and the Gaffers moved off too. The sun was down, and "damps" are bad for "rheumatics."

"It's a strange tale," said Gaffer II., "but if all's true ye tell me, there's not too many like him."

"That's right enough," Gaffer I. admitted. "He's been t' same all through, and ye should ha' seen the burying he gave t' ould chap. He was rare and good to him by all accounts, and never gainsaid him ought, except i' not lifting his voice as he should ha' done at t' grave. Jack sings a bass solo as well as any man i' t' place; but he stood yonder, for all t' world like one of them crows, black o' visage, and black wi' funeral clothes, and choked with crying like a child i'stead of a man."

"Well, well, t' ould chap were all he had, I reckon," said Gaffer II.

"*That's* right enough; and for going backwards, as ye may say, and setting a wild graff on an old standard, yon will's done well for DADDY DARWIN'S DOVECOT."

LOB LIE-BY-THE-FIRE;

OR,

THE LUCK OF LINGBOROUGH.

LOB LIE-BY-THE-FIRE.

INTRODUCTORY.

LOB LIE-BY-THE-FIRE—the Lubber-fiend, as Milton calls
him—is a rough kind of Brownie or House Elf, supposed
to haunt some north-country homesteads, where he does
the work of the farm labourers, for no grander wages than

> " —— to earn his cream-bowl duly set."

Not that he is insensible of the pleasures of rest, for

> " —— When, in one night, ere glimpse of morn,
> His shadowy flail hath threshed the corn
> That ten day-labourers could not end,
> Then lies him down the Lubber-fiend,
> And, stretched out all the chimney's length,
> Basks at the fire his hairy strength."

It was said that a Lob Lie-by-the-fire once haunted the
little old Hall at Lingborough. It was an old stone house
on the Borders, and seemed to have got its tints from the
grey skies that hung above it. It was cold-looking without, but cosy within, "like a north-country heart," said
Miss Kitty, who was a woman of sentiment, and kept a
commonplace book.

It was long before Miss Kitty's time that Lob Lie-by-the-fire first came to Lingborough. Why and whence he came is not recorded, nor when and wherefore he withdrew his valuable help, which, as wages rose, and prices rose also, would have been more welcome than ever.

This tale professes not to record more of him than comes within the memory of man.

Whether (as Fletcher says) he were the son of a witch, if curds and cream won his heart, and new clothes put an end to his labours, it does not pretend to tell. His history is less known than that of any other sprite. It may be embodied in some oral tradition that shall one day be found; but as yet the mists of forgetfulness hide it from the story-teller of to-day as deeply as the sea fogs are wont to lie between Lingborough and the adjacent coast.

THE LITTLE OLD LADIES.—ALMS DONE IN SECRET.

The little old ladies of Lingborough were heiresses.

Not, mind you, in the sense of being the children of some mushroom millionaire, with more money than manners, and (as Miss Betty had seen with her own eyes, on the daughter of a manufacturer who shall be nameless) dresses so fine in quality and be-furbelowed in construction as to cost a good quarter's income (of the little old ladies), but trailed in the dirt from "beggarly extravagance," or kicked out behind at every step by feet which fortune (and a very large fortune, too) had never taught to walk properly.

"And how should she know how to walk?" said Miss Betty. "Her mother can't have taught her, poor body! that ran through the streets of Leith, with a creel on her back, as a lassie ; and got out of her coach (lined with satin, you mind, sister Kitty ?) to her dying day, with a bounce, all in a heap, her dress caught, and her stockings exposed (among ourselves, ladies !) like some good wife that's afraid to be late for the market. Aye, aye ! Malcolm Midden—good man !—made a fine pocket of silver in a dirty trade, but his women'll jerk, and toss, and bounce, and fuss, and fluster for a generation or two yet, for all the silks and satins he can buy 'em."

From this it will be seen that the little old ladies inherited some prejudices of their class, and were also endowed with a shrewdness of observation common among all classes of north-country women.

But to return to what else they inherited. They were heiresses, as the last representatives of a family as old in that Border country as the bold blue hills which broke its horizon. They were heiresses also in default of heirs male to their father, who got the land from his uncle's dying childless—sons being scarce in the family. They were heiresses, finally, to the place and the farm, to the furniture that was made when folk seasoned their wood before they worked it, to a diamond brooch which they wore by turns, besides two diamond rings, and two black lace shawls, that had belonged to their mother and their Auntie Jean, long since departed thither where neither moth nor rust corrupt the true riches.

As to the incomings of Lingborough, " It was nobody's business but their own," as Miss Betty said to the lawyer who was their man of business, and whom they consulted on little matters of rent and repairs at as much length, and with as much formal solemnity, as would have gone else-where to the changing hands of half a million of money. Without violating their confidence, however, we may say that the estate paid its way, kept them in silk stockings, and gave them new tabbinet dresses once in three years.

It supplied their wants the better that they had inherited house plenishing from their parents, "which they thanked their stars was not made of tag-rag, and would last their time," and that they were quite content with an old home and old neighbours, and never desired to change the grand air that blew about their native hills for worse, in order to be poisoned with bad butter, and make the fortunes of extortionate lodging-house keepers.

The rental of Lingborough did more. How much more the little old ladies did not know themselves, and no one else shall know, till that which was done in secret is proclaimed from the housetops.

For they had had a religious scruple, founded upon a literal reading of the scriptural command that a man's left hand should not know what his right hand gives in alms, and this scruple had been ingeniously set at rest by the parson, who, failing in an attempt to explain the force of eastern hyperbole to the little ladies' satisfaction, had said that Miss Betty, being the elder, and the head of the house, might be likened to the right hand, and Miss Kitty, as the younger, to the left, and that if they pursued their good works without ostentation, or desiring the applause even of each other, the spirit of the injunction would be fulfilled.

The parson was a good man and a clever. He had (as Miss Betty justly said) a very spiritual piety. But he was also gifted with much shrewdness in dealing with the various members of his flock. And his word was law to the sisters.

Thus it came about that the little ladies' charities were not known even to each other—that Miss Betty turned her morning camlet twice instead of once, and Miss Kitty denied herself in sugar, to carry out benevolent little projects which were accomplished in secret, and of which no record appears in the Lingborough Ledger.

The little ladies of Lingborough were very sociable, and there was, as they said, " as much gaiety as was good for anyone" within their reach. There were at least six houses at which they drank tea from time to time, all within a walk. As hosts or guests, you always met the same people, which was a friendly arrangement, and the programmes of the entertainments were so uniform, that no one could possibly feel awkward. The best of manners and home-made wines distinguished these tea parties, where the company was strictly genteel, if a little faded. Supper was served at nine, and the parson and the lawyer played whist for love with different partners on different evenings with strict impartiality.

Small jealousies are apt to be weak points in small societies, but there was a general acquiescence in the belief that the parson had a friendly preference for the little ladies of Lingborough.

He lived just beyond them, too, which led to his invariably escorting them home. Miss Betty and Miss Kitty would not for worlds have been so indelicate as to take this attention for granted, though it was a custom of many years' standing. The older sister always went through the form of asking the younger to "see if the servant had come," and at this signal the parson always bade the lady of the house good-night, and respectfully proffered his services as an escort to Lingborough.

It was a lovely evening in June, when the little ladies took tea with the widow of General Dunmaw at her cottage, not quite two miles from their own home.

It was a memorable evening. The tea party was an agreeable one. The little ladies had new tabbinets on, and Miss Kitty wore the diamond brooch. Miss Betty had played whist with the parson, and the younger sister (perhaps because of the brooch) had been favoured with a good deal of conversation with the lawyer. It was an

honour, because the lawyer bore the reputation of an *esprit
fort*, and was supposed to have, as a rule, a contempt for
feminine intellects, which good manners led him to veil
under an almost officious politeness in society.   But
honours are apt to be uneasy blessings, and this one was at
least as harassing as gratifying.   For a somewhat monoto-
nous vein of sarcasm, a painful power of producing puns,
and a dexterity in suggesting doubts of everything, were
the main foundation of his intellectual reputation, and Miss
Kitty found them hard to cope with.   And it was a warm
evening.

But women have much courage, especially to defend a
friend or a faith, and the less Miss Kitty found herself
prepared for the conflict the harder she esteemed it her
duty to fight.   She fought for Church and State, for
parsons and poor people, for the sincerity of her friends,
the virtues of the Royal Family, the merit of Dr. Drugson's
prescriptions, and for her favourite theory that there is
some good in everyone and some happiness to be found
everywhere.

She rubbed nervously at the diamond brooch with her
thin little mittened hands.   She talked very fast ; and if
the lawyer were guilty of feeling any ungallant indifference
to her observations, she did not so much as hear his, and her
cheeks became so flushed that Mrs. Dunmaw crossed the
room in her China crape shawl and said, " My dear Miss
Kitty, I'm sure you feel the heat very much.   Do take my
fan, which is larger than yours."

But Miss Kitty was saved a reply, for at this moment
Miss Betty turned on the sofa, and said, " Dear Kitty, will
you kindly see if the servant——"

And the parson closed the volume of " Friendship's
Offering " which lay before him, and advanced towards Mrs.
Dunmaw and took leave in his own dignified way.

Miss Kitty was so much flustered that she had not even

presence of mind to look for the servant, who had never been ordered to come, but the parson relieved her by saying in his round, deep voice, " I hope you will not refuse me the honour of seeing you home, since our roads happen to lie together." And she was glad to get into the fresh air, and beyond the doubtful compliments of the lawyer's nasal suavity—"You have been very severe upon me to-night, Miss Kitty. I'm sure I had no notion I should find so powerful an antagonist," &c.

MIDSUMMER EVE.—A LOST DIAMOND.

It was Midsummer Eve. The long light of the North was pale and clear, and the western sky shone luminous through the fir-wood that bordered the road. Under such dim lights colours deepen, and the great bushes of broom, that were each one mass of golden blossom, blazed like fairy watch-fires up the lane.

Miss Kitty leaned on the left arm of the parson and Miss Betty on his right. She chatted gaily, which left her younger sister at leisure to think of all the convincing things she had not remembered to say to the lawyer, as the evening breeze cooled her cheeks.

" A grand prospect for the crops, sir," said Miss Betty ; " I never saw the broom so beautiful." But as she leaned forward to look at the yellow blaze which foretells good luck to farmers, as it shone in the hedge on the left-hand side of the road, she caught sight of the brooch in Miss Kitty's lace shawl. Through a gap in the wood the light from the western sky danced among the diamonds. But where one of the precious stones should have been, there was a little black hole.

"Sister, you've lost a stone out of your brooch !" screamed Miss Betty. The little ladies were well-trained, and even in that moment of despair Miss Betty would not hint that her sister's ornaments were not her sole property.

When Miss Kitty burst into tears the parson was a little astonished as well as distressed. Men are apt to be so, not perhaps because women cry on such very small accounts, as because the full reason does not always transpire. Tears are often the climax of nervous exhaustion, and this is commonly the result of more causes than one. Ostensibly Miss Kitty was "upset" by the loss of the diamond, but she also wept away a good deal of the vexation of her unequal conflict with the sarcastic lawyer, and of all this the parson knew nothing.

Miss Betty knew nothing of that, but she knew enough of things in general to feel sure that the diamond was not all the matter.

"What is amiss, sister Kitty?" said she. "Have you hurt yourself? Do you feel ill? Did you know the stone was out?"—"I hope you're not going to be hysterical, sister Kitty," added Miss Betty anxiously; "there never was a hysterical woman in our family yet."

"Oh dear no, sister Betty," sobbed Miss Kitty; "but it's all my fault. I know I was fidgeting with it whilst I was talking; and it's a punishment on my fidgety ways, and for ever presuming to wear it at all, when you're the head of the family, and solely entitled to it. And I shall never forgive myself if it's lost, and if it's found I'll never, never wear it any more." And as she deluged her best company pocket-handkerchief (for the useful one was in a big pocket under her dress, and could not be got at, the parson being present), Church, State, the Royal Family, the family Bible, her highest principles, her dearest affections, and the diamond brooch, all seemed to swim before her disturbed mind in one sea of desolation.

There was not a kinder heart than the parson's towards

"A grand prospect for the crops, sir," said Miss Betty; "I never saw the broom so beautiful."

women and children in distress.   He tucked the little
ladies again under his arms, and insisted upon going back
to Mrs. Dunmaw's, searching the lane as they went.   In
the pulpit or the drawing-room a ready anecdote never
failed him, and on this occasion he had several.   Tales of
lost rings, and even single gems, recovered in the most
marvellous manner and the most unexpected places—dug
up in gardens, served up to dinner in fishes, and so forth.
" Never," said Miss Kitty, afterwards, " never, to her dying
day, could she forget his kindness."

She clung to the parson as a support under both her
sources of trouble, but Miss Betty ran on and back, and
hither and thither, looking for the diamond.   Miss Kitty
and the parson looked too, and how many aggravating
little bits of glass and silica, and shining nothings and
good-for-nothings there are in the world, no one would
believe who has not looked for a lost diamond on a high
road.

But another story of found jewels was to be added to
the parson's stock.   He had bent his long back for about
the eighteenth time, when such a shimmer as no glass or
silica can give flashed into his eyes, and he caught up the
diamond out of the dust, and it fitted exactly into the little
black hole.

Miss Kitty uttered a cry, and at the same moment Miss
Betty, who was farther down the road, did the same, and
these were followed by a third, which sounded like a mock-
ing echo of both.   And then the sisters rushed together.

" A most miraculous discovery ! " gasped Miss Betty.

"You must have passed the very spot before," cried
Miss Kitty.

" Though I'm sure, sister, what to do with it now we
have found it I don't know," said Miss Betty, rubbing her
nose, as she was wont to do when puzzled.

" It shall be taken better care of for the future, sister

Betty," said Miss Kitty, penitently. "Though how it got out I can't think now."

"Why, bless my soul! you don't suppose it got there of itself, sister?" snapped Miss Betty. "How it did get there is another matter."

"I felt pretty confident about it, for my own part," smiled the parson as he joined them.

"Do you mean to say, sir, that you knew it was there?" asked Miss Betty, solemnly.

"I didn't know the precise spot, my dear madam, but——"

"You didn't see it, sir, I hope?" said Miss Betty.

"Bless me, my dear madam, I found it!" cried the parson.

Miss Betty bridled and bit her lip.

"I never contradict a clergyman, sir," said she, "but I can only say that if you did see it, it was not like your usual humanity to leave it lying there."

"Why { I've got it in my hand, ma'am!"
{ He's got it in his hand, sister!"

cried the parson and Miss Kitty in one breath. Miss Betty was too much puzzled to be polite.

"What are you talking about?" she asked.

"The diamond, oh dear, oh dear! *The diamond!*" cried Miss Kitty. "But what are you talking about, sister?"

"*The Baby*," said Miss Betty.

What Miss Betty Found.

It was found under a broom-bush. Miss Betty was poking her nose near the bank that bordered the wood, in her hunt for the diamond, when she caught sight of a mass of yellow of a deeper tint than the mass of broom-blossom above it, and this was the baby.

I

This vivid colour, less opaque than "deep chrome" and
a shade more orange, seems to have a peculiar attraction
for wandering tribes.   Gipsies use it, and it is a favourite
colour with Indian squaws.   To the last dirty rag it is
effective, whether it flutters near a tent on Bagshot Heath,
or in some wigwam doorway makes a point of brightness
against the grey shadows of the pine forest.

A large kerchief of this, wound about its body, was the
baby's only robe, but he seemed quite comfortable in it
when Miss Betty found him, sleeping on a pillow of deep
hair moss, his little brown fists closed as fast as his eyes,
and a crimson toadstool grasped in one of them.

When Miss Betty screamed the baby awoke, and his
long black lashes tickled his cheeks and made him wink
and cry.   But by the time she returned with her sister and

the parson, he was quite happy again, gazing up with dark
eyes full of delight into the glowing broom-bush, and fighting the evening breeze with his feet, which were entangled
in the folds of the yellow cloth, and with the battered toadstool which was still in his hand.

"And, indeed, sir," said Miss Betty, who had rubbed her
nose till it looked like the twin toadstool to that which the
baby was flourishing in her face, "you won't suppose I
would have left the poor little thing another moment, to
catch its death of cold on a warm evening like this; but
having no experience of such cases, and remembering that
murder at the inn in the Black Valley, and that the body
was not allowed to be moved till the constables had seen
it, I didn't feel to know how it might be with foundlings,
and——"

But still Miss Betty did not touch the bairn. She was
not accustomed to children. But the parson had christened
too many babies to be afraid of them, and he picked up the
little fellow in a moment, and tucked the yellow rag round
him, and then addressing the little ladies precisely as if
they were sponsors, he asked in his deep round voice,
"Now where on the face of the earth are the vagabonds
who have deserted this child?"

The little ladies did not know, the broom-bushes were
silent, and the question has remained unanswered from
that day to this.

The Baby, the Lawyer, and the Parson.

There were no railways near Lingborough at this time.
The coach ran three times a week, and a walking postman
brought the letters from the town to the small hamlets.
Telegraph wires were unknown, and yet news travelled
quite as fast then as it does now, and in the course of the

following morning all the neighbourhood knew that Miss
Betty had found a baby under a broom-bush, and the
lawyer called in the afternoon to inquire how the ladies
found themselves after the tea party at Mrs. General
Dunmaw's.

Miss Kitty was glad on the whole. She felt nervous,
but ready for a renewal of hostilities. Several clinching
arguments had occurred to her in bed last night, and after
hastily looking up a few lines from her common-place book,
which always made her cry when she read them, but which
she hoped to be able to hurl at the lawyer with a steady
voice, she followed Miss Betty to the drawing-room.

It was half a relief and half a disappointment to find
that the lawyer was quite indifferent to the subject of their
late contest. He overflowed with compliments ; was quite
sure he must have had the worst of the argument, and
positively dying of curiosity to hear about the baby.

The little ladies were very full of the subject themselves.
An active search for the baby's relations, conducted by the
parson, the clerk, the farm-bailiff, the constable, the cowherd, and several supernumeraries, had so far proved quite
vain. The country folk were most anxious to assist,
especially by word of mouth. Except a small but sturdy
number who had seen nothing, they had all seen "tramps,"
but unluckily no two could be got together whose accounts
of the tramps themselves, of the hour at which they were
seen, or of the direction in which they went, would tally
with each other.

The little ladies were quite alive to the possibility that
the child's parents might never be traced, indeed the matter
had been constantly before their minds ever since the
parson had carried the baby to Lingborough, and laid it in
the arms of Thomasina, the servant.

Miss Betty had sat long before her toilette-table that
evening, gazing vacantly at the looking-glass. Not that

the reflection of the eight curl-papers she had neatly twisted up was conveyed to her brain. She was in a brown study, during which the following thoughts passed through her mind, and they all pointed one way :

That that fine little fellow was not to blame for his people's misconduct.

That they would never be found.

That it would probably be the means of the poor child's ruin, body and soul, if they were.

That the master of the neighbouring workhouse bore a bad character.

That a child costs nothing to keep—where cows are kept too—for years.

That just at the age when a boy begins to eat dreadfully and wear out his clothes, he is very useful on a farm (though not for these reasons).

That Thomasina had taken to him.

That there need be no nonsense about it, as he could be brought up in his proper station in life in the kitchen and the farm-yard.

That tramps have souls.

That he would be taught to say his prayers.

Miss Betty said hers, and went to bed ; but all through that midsummer night the baby kept her awake, or flaunted his yellow robe and crimson toadstool through her dreams.

The morning brought no change in Miss Betty's views, but she felt doubtful as to how her sister would receive them. Would she regard them as foolish and unpractical, and her respect for Miss Betty's opinion be lessened thenceforward ?

The fear was needless. Miss Kitty was romantic and imaginative. She had carried the baby through his boy-hood about the Lingborough fields whilst she was dressing ; and he was attending her own funeral in the capacity of an attached and faithful servant, in black livery with worsted

frogs, as she sprinkled salt on her buttered toast at breakfast, when she was startled from this affecting day-dream
by Miss Betty's voice.

"Dear sister Kitty, I wish to consult you as to our plans
in the event of those wicked people who deserted the baby
not being found."

The little ladies resolved that not an inkling of their
benevolent scheme must be betrayed to the lawyer. But
they dissembled awkwardly, and the tone in which they
spoke of the tramp-baby roused the lawyer's quick sus-
picions. He had a real respect for the little ladies, and was
kindly anxious to save them from their own indiscretion.

"My dear ladies," said he, "I do hope your benevolence
—may I say your romantic benevolence?—of disposition is
not tempting you to adopt this gipsy waif?"

"I hope we know what is due to ourselves, and to the
estate—small, as it is—sir" said Miss Betty, "as well as to
Providence, too well to attempt to raise any child, however
handsome, from that station of life in which he was born."

"Bless me, madam! I never dreamed you would adopt
a beggar child as your heir; but I hope you mean to send
it to the workhouse, if the gipsy tramps it belongs to are
not to be found?"

"We have not made up our minds, sir, as to the course
we propose to pursue," said Miss Betty, with outward
dignity proportioned to her inward doubts.

"My dear ladies," said the lawyer anxiously, "let me
implore you not to be rash. To adopt a child in the most
favourable circumstances is the greatest of risks. But if
your benevolence *will* take that line, pray adopt some little
boy out of one of your tenants' families. Even your
teaching will not make him brilliant, as he is likely to
inherit the minimum of intellectual capacity; but he will
learn his catechism, probably grow up respectable, and
possibly grateful, since his forefathers have (so Miss Kitty

assures me) had all these virtues for generations.   But
this baby is the child of a heathen, barbarous, and wandering race.   The prospensities of the vagabonds who have
deserted him are in every drop of his blood.   All the
parsons in the diocese won't make a Christian of him, and
when (after anxieties I shudder to foresee) you flatter your-
selves that he is civilised, he will run away and leave his
shoes and stockings behind him."

"He has a soul to be saved, if he is a gipsy," said Miss
Kitty, hysterically.

"The soul, my dear Miss Kitty"—began the lawyer,
facing round upon her.

"Don't say anything dreadful about the soul, sir, I beg,"
said Miss Betty, firmly.   And then she added in a con-
ciliatory tone, "Won't you look at the little fellow, sir?   I
have no doubt his relations are shocking people ; but when
you see his innocent little face and his beautiful eyes, I
think you'll say yourself that if he were a duke's son he
couldn't be a finer child."

"My experience of babies is so limited, Miss Betty,"
said the lawyer, "that really—if you'll excuse me—but I
can quite imagine him.   I have before now been tempted
myself to adopt stray—puppies, when I have seen them in
the round, soft, innocent, bright-eyed stage.   And when
they have grown up in the hands of more credulous friends
into lanky, ill-conditioned, misconducted curs, I have con-
gratulated myself that I was not misled by the graces of
an age at which ill-breeding is less apparent than later in
life."

The little ladies both rose.   "If you see no difference,
sir," said Miss Betty in her stateliest manner, "between a
babe with an immortal soul and the beasts that perish, it is
quite useless to prolong the conversation."

"Reason is apt to be useless when opposed to the
generous impulses of a sex so full of sentiment as yours,

madam," said the lawyer, rising also. " Permit me to take
a long farewell, since it is improbable that our friendship
will resume its old position until your *protegé* has—run
away."

The words " long farewell " and " old friendship " were
quite sufficient to soften wrath in the tender hearts of the

little ladies. But the lawyer had really lost his temper,
and, before Miss Betty had decided how to offer the olive
branch without conceding her principles he was gone.

The weather was warm. The little ladies were heated
by discussion and the parson by vain scouring of the
country on foot, when they asked his advice upon their
project, and related their conversation with the lawyer.

The two gentlemen had so little in common that the parson felt it his duty not to let his advice be prejudiced by this fact. For some moments he sat silent, then he began to walk about as if he were composing a sermon ; then he stopped before the little ladies (who were sitting as stiffly on the sofa as if it were a pew) and spoke as if he were delivering one.

" If you ask me, dear ladies, whether it is your duty to provide for this child because you found him, I say that there is no such obligation. If you ask if I think it wise in your own interests, and hopeful as to the boy's career, I am obliged to agree with your legal adviser. Vagabond ways are seldom cured in one generation, and I think it is quite probable that, after much trouble and anxiety spent upon him, he may go back to a wandering life. But, Miss Betty," continued the parson in deepening tones, as he pounded his left palm with his right fist for want of a pulpit, " If you ask me whether I believe any child of any race is born incapable of improvement, and beyond benefit from the charities we owe to each other, I should deny my faith if I could say yes. I shall not, madam, confuse the end of your connection with him with the end of your training in him, even if he runs away, or fancy that I see the one because I see the other. I do not pretend to know how much evil he inherits from his forefathers as accurately as our graphic friend ; but I do know that he has a Father Whose image is also to be found in His children—not quite effaced in any of them—and Whose care of this one will last when yours, madam, may seem to have been in vain."

As the little ladies rushed forward and each shook a hand of the parson, he felt some compunction for his speech.

" I fear I am encouraging you in grave indiscretion," said he. " But, indeed, my dear ladies, I am quite against your project, for you do not realise the anxieties and disappointments that are before you, I am sure. The child will give you infinite trouble. I think he will run away. And yet I cannot in good conscience say that I believe love's labour must be lost. He may return to the woods and wilds ; but I hope he will carry something with him."

"Did the reverend gentleman mean Miss Betty's tea-spoons ?" asked the lawyer, stroking his long chin, when he was told what the parson had said.

BABYHOOD.—PRETTY FLOWERS.—THE ROSE-COLOURED TULIPS.

The matter of the baby's cap disturbed the little ladies. It seemed so like the beginning of a fulfilment of the lawyer's croakings.

Miss Kitty had made it. She had never seen a baby without a cap before, and the sight was unusual, if not indecent. But Miss Kitty was a quick needlewoman, and when the new cap was fairly tied over the thick crop of silky black hair, the baby looked so much less like Puck, and so much more like the rest of the baby world, that it was quite a relief.

Miss Kitty's feelings may therefore be imagined when, going to the baby just after the parson's departure, she found him in open rebellion against his cap. It had been tied on whilst he was asleep, and his eyes were no sooner open than he commenced the attack. He pulled with one little brown hand and tugged with the other ; he dragged a rosette over his nose and got the frills into his eyes ; he worried it as a puppy worries your handkerchief if you tie it round its face and tell it to "look like a grandmother."

At last the strings gave way, and he cast it triumphantly out of the clothes-basket which served him for cradle.

Successive efforts to induce him to wear it proved vain, so Thomasina said the weather was warm and his hair was very thick, and she parted this and brushed it, and Miss Kitty gave the cap to the farm bailiff's baby, who took to it as kindly as a dumpling to a pudding-cloth.

How the boy was ever kept inside his christening clothes, Thomasina said she did not know. But when he got into the parson's arms he lay quite quiet, which was a good omen. That he might lack no advantage, Miss Betty stood godmother for him, and the parish clerk and the sexton were his godfathers.

He was named John.

" A plain, sensible name," said Miss Betty. " And while we are about it," she added, " we may as well choose his surname. For a surname he must have, and the sooner it is decided upon the better.

Miss Kitty had made a list of twenty-seven of her favourite Christian names, which Miss Betty had sternly rejected, that everything might be plain, practical, and respectable at the outset of the tramp child's career. For the same reason she refused to adopt Miss Kitty's suggestions for a surname.

" It's so seldom there's a chance of *choosing* a surname for anybody, sister," said Miss Kitty, " it seems a pity not to choose a pretty one."

" Sister Kitty," said Miss Betty, " don't be romantic. The boy is to be brought up in that station of life for which one syllable is ample. I should have called him Smith if that had not been Thomasina's name. As it is, I propose to call him Broom. He was found under a bush of broom, and it goes very well with John, and sounds plain and respectable."

So Miss Betty bought a Bible, and on the fly-leaf of it

she wrote in her fine, round, gentlewoman's writing—"*John Broom. With good wishes for his welfare, temporal and eternal. From a sincere friend.*" And when the inscription was dry the Bible was wrapped in brown paper, and put by in Thomasina's trunk till John Broom should come to years of discretion.

He was slow to reach them, though in other respects he grew fast.

When he began to walk he would walk barefoot. To be out of doors was his delight, but on the threshold of the house he always sat down and discarded his shoes and stockings. Thomasina bastinadoed the soles of his feet with the soles of his shoes "to teach him the use of them," so she said. But Miss Kitty sighed, and thought of the lawyer's prediction.

There was no blinking the fact that the child was as troublesome as he was pretty. The very demon of mischief danced in his black eyes, and seemed to possess his feet and fingers as if with quicksilver. And if, as Thomasina said, you "never knew what he would be at next," you might also be pretty sure that it would be something he ought to have left undone.

John Broom early developed a taste for glass and crockery, and as the china cupboard was in that part of the house to which he by social standing also belonged, he had many chances to seize upon cups, jugs, and dishes. If detected with anything that he ought not to have had, it was his custom to drop the forbidden toy and toddle off as fast as his unpractised feet would carry him. The havoc which this caused amongst the glass and china was bewildering in a household where tea-sets and dinner-sets had passed from generation to generation, where slapdash, giddy-pated kitchenmaids never came, where Miss Betty washed the best teacups in the parlour, where Thomasina was more careful than her mistress, and the breaking of a

single plate was a serious matter, and, if beyond riveting, a
misfortune.

Thomasina soon found that her charge was safest, as he
was happiest, out of doors.   A very successful device was

to shut him up in the drying ground, and tell him to " pick the pretty flowers." John Broom preferred flowers even to china cups with gilding on them. He gathered nosegays of daisies and buttercups, and the winning way in which he would present these to the little ladies atoned, in their benevolent eyes, for many a smashed teacup.

But the tramp-baby's restless spirit was soon weary of the drying-ground, and he set forth one morning in search of "fresh woods and pastures new." He had seated himself on the threshold to take off his shoes, when he heard the sound of Thomasina's footsteps, and, hastily staggering to his feet, toddled forth without farther delay. The sky was blue above him, the sun was shining, and the air was very sweet. He ran for a bit and then tumbled, and picked himself up again, and got a fresh impetus, and so on till he reached the door of the kitchen garden, which was open. It was an old-fashioned kitchen-garden with flowers in the borders. There were single rose-coloured tulips which had been in the garden as long as Miss Betty could remember, and they had been so increased by dividing the clumps that they now stretched in two rich lines of colour down both sides of the long wall. And John Broom saw them.

" Pick the pretty f'owers, love," said he, in imitation of Thomasina's patronising tone, and forthwith beginning at the end, he went steadily to the top of the right-hand border, mowing the rose-coloured tulips as he went.

Meanwhile, when Thomasina came to look for him he could not be found, and when all the back premises and the drying-ground had been searched in vain, she gave the alarm to the little ladies.

Miss Kitty's vivid imagination leaped at once to the conclusion that the child's vagabond relations had fetched him away, and she became rigid with alarm. But Miss Betty rushed out into the shrubbery, and Miss Kitty took a whiff of her vinaigrette and followed her.

When they came at last to the kitchen-garden, Miss
Betty's grief for the loss of John Broom did not prevent
her observing that there was something odd about the
borders, and when she got to the top, and found that all
the tulips had been picked from one side, she sank down
on the roller which happened to be lying beside her.

And John Broom staggered up to her, and crying, "For
'oo, Miss Betty," fell headlong with a sheaf of rose-coloured
tulips into her lap.

As he did not offer any to Miss Kitty, her better judgment was not warped, and she said, "You must slap him,
sister Betty."

"Put out your hand, John Broom," said Miss Betty,
much agitated.

And John Broom, who was quite composed, put out
both his little grubby paws so trustfully that Miss Betty
had not the heart to strike him. But she scolded him,
"Naughty boy!" and she pointed to the tulips and shook

her head. John Broom looked thoughtfully at them, and shook his.

"Naughty boy!" repeated Miss Betty, and she added in very impressive tones, "John Broom's a very naughty boy!"

After which she took him to Thomasina, and Miss Kitty collected the rose-coloured tulips and put them into water in the best old china punch-bowl.

In the course of the afternoon she peeped into the kitchen, where John Broom sat on the floor, under the window, gazing thoughtfully up into the sky.

"As good as gold, bless his little heart!" murmured Miss Kitty. For as his feet were tucked under him, she did not know that he had just put his shoes and stockings into the pig-tub, into which he all but fell himself from the exertion. He did not hear Miss Kitty, and thought on. He wanted to be out again, and he had a tantalising remembrance of the ease with which the tender juicy stalks of the tulips went snap, snap, in that new place of amusement he had discovered. Thomasina looked into the kitchen and went away again. When she had gone, John Broom went away also.

He went both faster and steadier on his bare feet. And when he got into the kitchen garden, it recalled Miss Betty to his mind. And he shook his head, and said, "Naughty boy!" And then he went up the left-hand border, mowing the tulips as he went; after which he trotted home, and met Thomasina at the back door. And he hugged the sheaf of rose-coloured tulips in his arms, and said, "John Broom a very naughty boy!"

Thomasina was not sentimental, and she slapped him well—his hands for picking the tulips, and his feet for going bare-foot.

But his feet had to be slapped with Thomasina's slipper, for his own shoes could not be found.

Education.—Fireside Tales.

In spite of all his pranks, John Broom did not lose the favour of his friends. Thomasina spoiled him, and Miss Betty and Miss Kitty tried not to do so.

The parson had said, "Treat the child fairly. Bring him up as he will have to live hereafter. Don't make him half pet and half servant." And following this advice, and her own resolve that there should be "no nonsense" in the matter, Miss Betty had made it a rule that he should not be admitted to the parlour. It bore more heavily on the tender hearts of the little ladies than on the light heart of John Broom, and led to their waylaying him in the passages and gardens with little gifts, unknown to each other. And when Miss Kitty kissed his newly-washed cheeks, and pronounced them "like ripe russets," Miss Betty murmured, "Be judicious, sister Kitty;" and Miss Kitty would correct any possible ill effects by saying, "*Now* make your bow to your betters, John Broom, and say, 'Thank, you, ma'am!'" which was accomplished by the child's giving a tug to the forelock of his thick black hair, with a world of mischief in his eyes.

When he was old enough, the little ladies sent him to the village school.

The total failure of their hopes for his education was not the smallest of the disappointments Miss Betty and Miss Kitty endured on his behalf. The quarrel with the lawyer had been made up long ago, and though there was always a touch of raillery in his inquiries after "the young gipsy," he had once said, "If he turns out anything of a genius at school, I might find a place for him in the office, by-and-by." The lawyer was kind-hearted in his own fashion, and on this hint Miss Kitty built up hopes, which unhappily were met by no responsive ambition in John Broom.

K

As to his fitness to be an errand boy, he could not carry a message from the kitchen to the cowhouse without stop_ping by the way to play with the yard-dog, and a hedgehog in the path would probably have led him astray, if Thomasina had had a fit and he had been despatched for the doctor.

During school hours he spent most of his time under the fool's-cap when he was not playing truant.   With his schoolmates he was good friends.   If he was seldom out of mischief, he was seldom out of temper.   He could beat any boy at a foot race (without shoes) ; he knew the notes and nests of every bird that sang, and whatever an old pocket-knife is capable of, that John Broom could and would do with it for his fellows.

Miss Betty had herself tried to teach him to read, and she continued to be responsible for his religious instruction. She had hoped to stir up his industry by showing him the Bible, and promising that when he could read it he should have it for his "very own."   But he either could not or would not apply himself, so the prize lay unearned in Thomasina's trunk.   But he would listen for any length of time to Scripture stories, if they were read or told to him, especially to the history of Elisha, and the adventures of the Judges.

Indeed, since he could no longer be shut up in the dry-ing ground, Thomasina had found that he was never so happy and so safe as when he was listening to tales, and many a long winter evening he lay idle on the kitchen hearth, with his head on the sheep dog, whilst the more industrious Thomasina plied her knitting-needles, as she sat in the ingle-nook, with the flickering firelight playing among the plaits of her large cap, and told tales of the country side.

Not that John Broom was her only hearer.   Annie " the lass " sat by the hearth also, and Thomasina took care tha* she did not "sit with her hands before her." And a little farther away sat the cowherd.

He had a sleeping-room above the barn, and took his meals in the house. By Miss Betty's desire he always went in to family prayers after supper, when he sat as close as possible to the door, under an uncomfortable conscious- ness that Thomasina did not think his boots clean enough for the occasion, and would find something to pick off the carpet as she followed him out, however hardly he might have used the door-scraper beforehand.

It might be a difficult matter to decide which he liked best, beer or John Broom. But next to these he liked Thomasina's stories.

Thomasina was kind to him. With all his failings and the dirt on his boots, she liked him better than the farm-bailiff. The farm-bailiff was thrifty and sensible and faith- ful, and Thomasina was faithful and sensible and thrifty, and they each had a tendency to claim the monopoly of those virtues. Notable people complain, very properly, of thriftless and untidy ones, but they sometimes agree better with them than with rival notabilities. And so Thomasina's broad face beamed benevolently as she bid the cowherd "draw up" to the fire, and he who (like Thomasina) was a native of the country, would confirm the marvels she related, with a proper pride in the wonderful district to which they both belonged.

He would help her out sometimes with names and dates in a local biography. By his own account he knew the man who was murdered at the inn in the Black Valley so intimately that it turned Annie the lass as white as a dish- cloth to sit beside him. If Thomasina said that folk were yet alive who had seen the little green men dance in Dawborough Croft, the cowherd would smack his knees and cry, "Scores on 'em!" And when she whispered of the white figure which stood at the cross roads after midnight, he testified to having seen it himself—tall beyond mortal height, and pointing four ways at once. He had a legend of his own too, which Thomasina sometimes gave him the chance of telling, of how he was followed home one moonlight night by a black Something as big as a young calf, which "wimmled and wammled" around him till he fell senseless into the ditch, and being found there by the farm-bailiff on his return from market, was unjustly accused of the vice of intoxication.

"Fault-finders should be free of flaws," Thomasina would say with a prim chin. She *had* seen the farm-bailiff himself "the worse" for more than his supper beer.

But there was one history which Thomasina was always loth to relate, and it was that which both John Broom and the cowherd especially preferred—the history of Lob Lie-by-the-fire.

Thomasina had a feeling (which was shared by Annie the lass) that it was better not to talk of "anything" peculiar to the house in which you are living. One's neighbours' ghosts and bogles are another matter.

But to John Broom and the cowherd no subject was so interesting as that of the Lubber-fiend. The cowherd sighed to think of the good old times when a man might sleep on in spite of cocks, and the stables be cleaner, and the beasts better tended than if he had been up with the lark. And John Broom's curiosity was never quenched about the rough, hairy Good-fellow who worked at night that others might be idle by day, and who was sometimes caught at his hard-earned nap, lying, "like a great hurgin bear," where the boy loved to lie himself, before the fire, on this very hearth.

Why and where he had gone, Thomasina could not tell. She had heard that he had originally come from some other household, where he had been offended. But whether he had gone elsewhere when he forsook Lingborough, or whether "such things had left the country" for good, she did not pretend to say.

And when she had told, for the third or fourth time, how his porridge was put into a corner of the cowhouse for him overnight, and how he had been often overheard at his work, but rarely seen, and then only lying before the fire, Miss Betty would ring for prayers, and Thomasina would fold up her knitting and lead the way, followed by Annie the lass, whose nerves John Broom would startle by treading on her heels, the rear being brought up by the cowherd, looking hopelessly at his boots.

Miss Betty and Miss Kitty did really deny themselves the indulgence of being indulgent, and treated John Broom on principles, and for his good. But they did so in their own tremulous and spasmodic way, and got little credit for it. Thomasina, on the other hand, spoiled him with such a masterful managing air, and so much sensible talk, that no one would have thought that the only system she followed was to conceal his misdemeanours; and to stand between him and the just wrath of the farm-bailiff.

The farm-bailiff, or grieve, as he liked to call himself, was a Scotchman, with a hard-featured face (which he washed on the Sabbath), a harsh voice, a good heart rather deeper down in his body than is usual, and a shrewd, money-getting head, with a speckled straw hat on the top of it. No one could venture to imagine when that hat was new, or how long ago it was that the farm-bailiff went to the expense of purchasing those work-day clothes. But the dirt on his face and neck was an orderly accumulation, such as gathers on walls, oil-paintings, and other places to which soap is not habitually applied ; it was not a matter of spills and splashes, like the dirt John Broom disgraced himself with. And his clothes, if old, fitted neatly about him ; they never suggested raggedness, which was the normal condition of the tramp-boy's jackets. They only

looked as if he had been born (and occasionally buried) in
them.   It is needful to make this distinction, that the good
man may not be accused of inconsistency in the peculiar
vexation which John Broom's disorderly appearance caused
him.

In truth, Miss Betty's *protegé* had reached the age at
which he was to "eat dreadfully, wear out his clothes, and
be useful on the farm ; " and the last condition was quite
unfulfilled.   At eleven years old he could not be trusted to
scare birds, and at half that age the farm-bailiff's eldest
child could drive cattle.

"And no' just ruin the leddies in new coats and compliments, either, like some ne'er-do-weels," added the farm-
bailiff, who had heard with a jealous ear of sixpences given
by Miss Betty and Miss Kitty to their wasteful favourite.

When the eleventh anniversary of John Broom's discovery was passed, and his character at school gave no hopes
of his ever qualifying himself to serve the lawyer, it was
resolved that—" idleness being the mother of mischief," he
should be put under the care of the farm-bailiff, to do such
odd jobs about the place as might be suited to his capacity
and love of outdoor life.   And now John Broom's troubles
began.   By fair means or foul, with here an hour's weeding
and there a day's bird scaring, and with errands perpetual,
the farm-bailiff contrived to "get some work out of" the
idle little urchin.   His speckled hat and grim face seemed
to be everywhere, and always to pop up when John Broom
began to play.

They lived "at daggers drawn."   I am sorry to say that
John Broom's fitful industry was still kept for his own
fancies.   To climb trees, to run races with the sheep dog,
to cut grotesque sticks, gather hedge fruits, explore a bog,
or make new friends among beasts and birds—at such
matters he would labour with feverish zeal.   But so far
from trying to cure himself of his indolence about daily

drudgery, he found a new and pleasant excitement in thwarting the farm-bailiff at every turn.

It would not sound dignified to say that the farm-bailiff took pleasure in thwarting John Broom. But he certainly did not show his satisfaction when the boy did do his work properly. Perhaps he thought that praise is not good for young people; and the child did not often give him the chance of trying. Of blame he was free enough. Not a good scolding to clear the air, such as Thomasina would give to Annie the lass, but his slow, caustic tongue was always growling, like muttered thunder, over John Broom's incorrigible head.

He had never approved of the tramp-child, who had the overwhelming drawbacks of having no pedigree and of being a bad bargain as to expense. This was not altogether John Broom's fault, but with his personal failings the farm-bailiff had even less sympathy. It had been hinted that he was born in the speckled hat, and whether this were so or not, he certainly had worn an old head whilst his shoulders were still young, and could not remember the time when he wished to waste his energies on anything that did not earn or at least save something.

Once only did anything like approval of the lad escape his lips.

Miss Betty's uncle's second cousin had returned from foreign lands with a good fortune and several white cockatoos. He kept the fortune himself, but he gave the cockatoos to his friends, and he sent one of them to the little ladies of Lingborough.

He was a lovely creature (the cockatoo, not the cousin, who was plain), and John Broom's admiration of him was boundless. He gazed at the sulphur-coloured crest, the pure white wings with their deeper-tinted lining, and even the beak and the fierce round eyes, as he had gazed at the broom-bush in his babyhood, with insatiable delight.

The cousin did things handsomely. He had had a ring put round one of the cockatoo's ankles, with a bright steel chain attached and a fastener to secure it to the perch. The cockatoo was sent in the cage by coach, and a perch, made of foreign wood, followed by the carrier.

Miss Betty and Miss Kitty were delighted both with the cockatoo and the perch, but they were a good deal troubled as to how to fasten the two together. There was a neat little ring on the perch, and the cockatoo's chain was quite complete, and he evidently wanted to get out, for he shook

the walls of his cage in his gambols.   But he put up his
crest and snapped when any one approached, in a manner
so alarming that Annie the lass shut herself up in the dairy,
and the farm-bailiff turned his speckled hat in his hands,
and gave cautious counsel from a safe distance.

"How he flaps!" cried Miss Betty.   "I'm afraid he **has**
a very vicious temper."

"He only wants to get out, Miss Betty," said John
Broom.   "He'd be all right with his perch, and I think I
can get him on it."

"Now Heaven save us from the sin o' presumption!"
cried the farm-bailiff, and putting on the speckled hat, he
added, slowly : "I'm thinking, John Broom, that if ye're
engaged wi' the leddies this morning it'll be time I turned
my hand to singling these few turnips ye've been thinking
about the week past."

On which he departed, and John Broom pressed the
little ladies to leave him alone with the bird.

"We shouldn't like to leave you alone with a wild
creature like that," said Miss Betty.

"He's just frightened on ye, Miss Betty.   He'll be like
a lamb when you're gone," urged John Broom.

"Besides, we should like to see you do it," said Miss
Kitty.

"You can look in through the window, miss.   I must
fasten the door, or he'll be out."

"I should never forgive myself if he hurt you, John," said
Miss Betty, irresolutely, for she was very anxious to have
the cockatoo and perch in full glory in the parlour.

"He'll none hurt me, miss," said John, with a cheerful
smile on his rosy face.   "I likes him, and he'll like me."

This settled the matter.   John was left with the cockatoo.   He locked the door, and the little ladies went into
the garden and peeped through the window.

They saw John Broom approach the cage, on which the

cockatoo put up his crest, opened his beak slowly, and snarled, and Miss Betty tapped on the window and shook her black satin workbag.

"Don't go near him!" she cried. But John Broom paid no attention.

"What are you putting up that top-knot of yours at me for?" said he to the cockatoo. "Don't ye know your own friends? I'm going to let ye out, I am. You're going on to your perch, you are."

"Eh, but you're a bonny creature!" he added, as the cockatoo filled the cage with snow and sulphur flutterings.

"Keep away, keep away!" screamed the little ladies, playing a duet on the window panes.

"Out with you!" said John Broom, as he unfastened the cage door.

And just when Miss Betty had run round, and as she shouted through the keyhole, "Open the door, John Broom. We've changed our minds. We've decided to keep it in its cage," the cockatoo strode solemnly forth on his eight long toes.

"Pretty Cocky!" said he.

When Miss Betty got back to the window, John Broom had just made an injudicious grab at the steel chain, on which Pretty Cocky flew fiercely at him, and John, burying his face in his arms, received the attack on his thick poll, laughing into his sleeves and holding fast to the chain, whilst the cockatoo and the little ladies screamed against each other.

"It'll break your leg—you'll tear its eyes out!" cried Miss Kitty.

"Miss Kitty means that you'll break its leg, and it will tear your eyes out," Miss Betty explained through the glass. "John Broom! Come away! Lock it in! Let it go!"

But Cocky was now waddling solemnly round the room,

and John Broom was creeping after him, with the end of
the chain in one hand, and the perch in the other, and in a
moment more he had joined the chain and the ring, and
just as Miss Betty was about to send for the constable and
have the door broken open, Cocky—driven into a corner—

clutched his perch and was raised triumphantly to his place
in the bow-window.

He was now a parlour pet, and John Broom saw little
of him. This vexed him, for he had taken a·passionate
liking for the bird. The little ladies rewarded him well for

his skill, but this brought him no favour from the farm-bailiff, and matters went on as ill as before.

One day the cockatoo got his chain entangled, and Miss Kitty promptly advanced to put it right. She had unfastened that end which secured it to the perch, when Cocky, who had been watching the proceedings with much interest, dabbed at her with his beak. Miss Kitty fled, but with great presence of mind shut the door after her. She forgot, however, that the window was open, in front of which stood the cockatoo scanning the summer sky with his fierce eyes, and flapping himself in the breeze.

And just as the little ladies ran into the garden, and Miss Kitty was saying, " One comfort is, sister Betty, that it's quite safe in the room, till we can think what to do next," he bowed his yellow crest, spread his noble wings, and sailed out into the æther.

In ten minutes the whole able-bodied population of the place was in the grounds of Lingborough, including the farm-bailiff.

The cockatoo was on the top of a fir-tree, and a fragment of the chain was with him, for he had broken it, and below on the lawn stood the little ladies, who, with the unfailing courage of women in a hopeless cause, were trying to dislodge him by waving their pocket-handkerchiefs and crying " sh ! "

He looked composedly down out of one eye for some time, and then he began to move.

" I think it's coming down now," said Miss Kitty.

But in a quarter of a minute, Cocky had sailed a quarter of a mile, and was rocking himself on the top of an old willow-tree. And at this moment John Broom joined the crowd which followed him.

" I'm thinking he's got his chain fast," said the farm-bailiff ; " if onybody that understood the beastie daured to get near him——"

"I'll get him," said John Broom, casting down his hat.

"Ye'll get your neck thrawed," said the farm-bailiff.

"We won't hear of it," said the little ladies.

But to their horror, John Broom kicked off his shoes, after which he spat upon his hands (a shock which Miss Kitty thought she never could have survived), and away he went up the willow.

It was not an easy tree to climb, and he had one or two narrow escapes, which kept the crowd breathless, but he shook the hair from his eyes, moistened his hands afresh, and went on. The farm-bailiff's far-away heart was stirred. No Scotchman is insensible to gallantry. And courage is the only thing a "canny" Scot can bear to see expended without return.

"John Broom," screamed Miss Betty, "come down! I order, I command you to come down."

The farm-bailiff drew his speckled hat forward to shade his upward gaze, and folded his arms.

"Dinna call on him, leddies," he said, speaking more quickly than usual. "Dinna mak him turn his head. Steady, lad! Grip wi' your feet. Spit on your pawms, man."

Once the boy trod on a rotten branch, and as he drew back his foot, and it came crashing down, the farm-bailiff set his teeth, and Miss Kitty fainted in Thomasina's arms.

"I'll reward anyone who'll fetch him down," sobbed Miss Betty. But John Broom seated himself on the same branch as the cockatoo, and undid the chain and prepared his hands for the downward journey.

"You've got a rare perch, this time," said he. And Pretty Cocky crept towards him, and rubbed its head against him and chuckled with joy.

What dreams of liberty in the tree tops, with John Broom for a playfellow, passed through his crested head, who shall say? But when he found that his friend meant to take him prisoner, he became very angry and much alarmed. And when John Broom grasped him by both legs and began to descend, Cocky pecked him vigorously. But the boy held the back of his head towards him, and went steadily down.

"Weel done!" roared the farm-bailiff. "Gently, lad! Gude save us! ha'e a care o' yoursen. That's weel. Keep your pow at him. Dinna let the beast get to your een."

But when John Broom was so near the ground as to be safe, the farm-bailiff turned wrathfully upon his son, who had been gazing open-mouthed at the sight which had so interested his father.

"Ye look weel standing gawping here, before the leddies," said he, "wasting the precious hours, and bringing your father's grey hairs wi' sorrow to the grave; and John Broom yonder shaming ye, and you not so much as thinking to fetch the perch for him, ye lazy loon. Away wi' ye and get it, before I lay a stick about your shoulders."

And when his son had gone for the perch, and John Broom was safely on the ground, laughing, bleeding, and triumphant, the farm-bailiff said,—

"Ye're a bauld chiel, John Broom, I'll say that for ye."

INTO THE MIST.

Unfortunately the favourable impression produced by "the gipsy lad's" daring soon passed from the farm-bailiff's mind. It was partly effaced by the old jealousy of the little ladies' favour. Miss Betty gave the boy no less than four silver shillings, and he ungraciously refused to let the farm-bailiff place them in a savings bank for him.

Matters got from bad to worse. The farming man was not the only one who was jealous, and John Broom himself was as idle and restless as ever. Though, if he had listened respectfully to the Scotchman's counsels, or shown any disposition to look up to and be guided by him, much might have been overlooked. But he made fun of him and made a friend of the cowherd. And this latter most manifest token of low breeding vexed the respectable taste of the farm-bailiff.

John Broom had his own grievances too, and he brooded

over them. He thought the little ladies had given him over to the farm-bailiff, because they had ceased to care for him, and that the farm-bailiff was prejudiced against him beyond any hope of propitiation. The village folk taunted him, too, with being an outcast, and called him Gipsy John, and this maddened him. Then he would creep into the cow-house and lie in the straw against the white cow's warm back, and for a few of Miss Betty's coppers, to spend in beer or tobacco, the cowherd would hide him from the farm-bailiff and tell him countryside tales. To Thomasina's stories of ghosts and gossips, he would add strange tales of smugglers on the near-lying coast, and as John Broom listened, his restless blood rebelled more and more against the sour sneers and dry drudgery that he got from the farm-bailiff.

Nor were sneers the sharpest punishment his misdemeanours earned. The farm-bailiff's stick was thick and his arm was strong, and he had a tendency to believe that if a flogging was good for a boy, the more he had of it the better it would be for him.

And John Broom, who never let a cry escape him at the time, would steal away afterwards and sob out his grief into the long soft coat of the sympathising sheep dog.

Unfortunately he never tried the effect of deserving better treatment as a remedy for his woes. The parson's good advice and Miss Betty's entreaties were alike in vain. He was ungrateful even to Thomasina. The little ladies sighed and thought of the lawyer. And the parson preached patience.

"Cocky has been tamed," said Miss Kitty, thoughtfully, "perhaps John Broom will get steadier by-and-by."

"It seems a pity we can't chain him to a perch, Miss Kitty," laughed the parson; "he would be safe then, at any rate."

Miss Betty said afterwards that it did seem so remarkable that the parson should have made this particular joke on this particular night—the night when John Broom did not come home.

He had played truant all day. The farm-bailiff had wanted him, and he had kept out of the way.

The wind was from the east, and a white mist rolled in from the sea, bringing a strange invigorating smell, and making your lips clammy with salt. It made John Broom's heart beat faster, and filled his head with dreams of ships and smugglers, and rocking masts higher than the willow-tree, and winds wilder than this wind, and dancing waves.

Then something loomed through the fog. It was the farm-bailiff's speckled hat. John Broom hesitated—the thick stick became visible.

Then a cloud rolled between them, and the child turned, and ran, and ran, and ran, coastwards, into the sea mist.

THE SEA.—THE ONE-EYED SAILOR.—THE OTHER SIDE OF THE WORLD.

John Broom was footsore when he reached the coast, but that keen, life-giving smell had drawn him on and held him up. The fog had cleared off, and he strained his black eyes through the darkness to see the sea.

He had never seen it—that other world within this, on which one lived out of doors, and climbed about all day, and no one blamed him.

When he did see it, he thought he had got to the end of the world. If the edge of the cliff were not the end, he could not make out where the sky began ; and if that darkness were the sea, the sea was full of stars.

But this was because the sea was quiet and reflected the colour of the night sky, and the stars were the lights of the herring-boats twinkling in the bay.

When he got down by the water he saw the vessels lying alongside, and they were dirtier than he had supposed. But he did not lose heart, and remembering, from the cowherd's tales, that people who cannot pay for their passage must either work it out or hide themselves on board ship, he took the easier alternative, and got on to the first vessel which had a plank to the quay, and hid himself under some tarpaulin on the deck.

The vessel was a collier bound for London, and she sailed with the morning tide.

L

When he was found out he was not ill-treated. Indeed, the rough skipper offered to take him home again on his return voyage. He would have liked to go, but pride withheld him, and home sickness had not yet eaten into his very soul. Then an old sailor with one eye (but that a sly one) met him, and told him tales more wonderful than the cowherd's. And with him he shipped as cabin - boy, on a vessel bound for the other side of the world.

* * * *

A great many sins bring their own punishment in this life pretty clearly, and sometimes pretty closely ; but few more directly or more bitterly than rebellion against the duties, and ingratitude for the blessings, of home.

There was no playing truant on board ship ; and as to the master poor John Broom served now, his cruelty made the memory of the farm-bailiff a memory of tenderness and gentleness and indulgence. Till he was half-naked and half-starved, and had only short snatches of sleep in hard corners, it had never struck him that when one has got good food and clothes, and sound sleep in a kindly home, he has got more than many people, and enough to be thankful for.

He did everything he was told now as fast as he could do it, in fear for his life. The one-eyed sailor had told him that the captain always took orphans and poor friendless lads to be his cabin-boys, and John Broom thought what a nice kind man he must be, and how different from the farm-bailiff, who thought nobody could be trustworthy unless he could show parents and grand-parents, and cousins to the sixth degree. But after they had sailed, when John Broom felt very ill, and asked the one-eyed sailor where he was to sleep, the one-eyed sailor pleasantly replied that if he hadn't brought a four-post bed in his pocket he must sleep where he could, for that all the other cabin-boys were sleeping in Davy's Locker, and couldn't be disturbed. And it was not till John Broom had learned ship's language that he found out that Davy's Locker meant the deep, and that the other cabin-boys were dead. "And as they'd nobody belonging to 'em, no hearts was broke," added the sailor, winking with his one eye.

John Broom slept standing sometimes for weariness, but he did not sleep in Davy's Locker. Young as he was he had dauntless courage, a careless hopeful heart, and a tough little body ; and that strong, life-giving sea smell bore him up instead of food, and he got to the other side of the world.

Why he did not stay there, why he did not run away into the wilderness to find at least some easier death than to have his bones broken by the cruel captain, he often wondered afterwards. He was so much quicker and braver than the boys they commonly got, that the old sailor kept a sharp watch over him with his one eye whilst they were ashore ; but one day he was too drunk to see out of it, and John Broom ran away.

It was Christmas Day, and so hot that he could not run far, for he was at the other side of the world, where things are upside down, and he sat down by the roadside on the outskirts of the city ; and as he sat, with his thin, brown face resting on his hands, a familiar voice beside him said, "Pretty Cocky!" and looking up he saw a man with several cages of birds. The speaker was a cockatoo of the most exquisite shades of cream-colour, salmon, and rose, and he had a rose-coloured crest. But lovely as he was, John Broom's eyes were on another cage, where, silent, solemn, and sulky, sat a big white one with sulphur-coloured trimmings and fierce black eyes ; and he was so like Miss Betty's pet, that the poor child's heart bounded as if a hand had been held out to him from home.

"If you let him get at you, you'll not do it a second time, mate," said the man. "He's the nastiest tempered beast I ever saw. I'd have rung his neck long ago if he hadn't such a fine coat.

But John Broom said, as he had said before, "I like him, and he'll like me."

When the cockatoo bit his finger to the bone, the man roared with laughter, but John Broom did not draw his hand away. He kept it still at the bird's beak, and with the other he gently scratched him under the crest and wings. And when the white cockatoo began to stretch out his eight long toes, as cats clutch with their claws from pleasure, and chuckled, and sighed, and bit softly without hurting, and laid his head against the bars till his snow and sulphur feathers touched John Broom's black locks, the man was amazed.

"Look here, mate," said he, "you've the trick with birds and no mistake. I'll sell you this one cheap, and you'll be able to sell him dear."

"I've not a penny in the world," said John Broom.

"You do look cleaned out, too," said the man, scanning him from head to foot. "I tell you what, you shall come with me a bit and tame the birds, and I'll find you something to eat."

Ten minutes before, John Broom would have jumped at
this offer, but now he refused it.   The sight of the cockatoo
had brought back the fever of home sickness in all its
fierceness.   He couldn't stay out here.   He would dare anything, do anything, to see the hills about Lingborough once
more before he died ; and even if he did not live to see

them, he might live to sleep in that part of Davy's Locker
which should rock him on the shores of home.

The man gave him a shilling for fastening a ring and
chain on to the Cocky's ankle, and with this he got the
best dinner he had eaten since he lost sight of the farm-
bailiff's speckled hat in the mist.

And then he went back to the one-eyed sailor, and
shipped as cabin-boy again for the homeward voyage.

THE HIGHLANDER.—BARRACK LIFE.—THE GREAT
CURSE.—JOHN BROOM'S MONEY-BOX.

When John Broom did get home he did not go to sea
again.   He lived from hand to mouth in the seaport town,
and slept, as he was well accustomed to sleep, in holes and
corners.

Every day and every night, through the long months of
the voyage, he had dreamed of begging his way barefoot
to Miss Betty's door.   But now he did not go.   His life
was hard, but it was not cruel.   He was very idle, and there
was plenty to see.   He wandered about the country as of
old.   The ships and shipping too had a fascination for him
now that the past was past, and here he could watch them
from the shore ; and, partly for shame and partly for pride,
he could not face the idea of going back.   If he had been
taunted with being a vagrant boy before, what would be
said now if he presented himself, a true tramp, to the farm-
bailiff?   Besides, Miss Betty and Miss Kitty could not
forgive him.   It was impossible !

He was wandering about one day when he came to some
fine high walls with buildings inside.   There was an open
gateway, at which stood a soldier with a musket.   But a
woman and some children went in, and he did not shoot
them ; so when his back was turned, and he was walking
stiffly to where he came from, John Broom ran in through
the gateway.

The first man he saw was the grandest-looking man he
had ever seen.   Indeed, he looked more like a bird than a
man—a big bird with a big black crest.   He was very tall.
His feet were broad and white, like the feathered feet of
some plumy bird, his legs were bare and brown and hairy.
He was clothed in many colours.   He had fur in front,
which swung as he walked, and silver and shining stones
about him.   He held his head very high, and from it

drooped great black plumes.   His face looked as if it had been cut—roughly but artistically—out of a block of old wood, and his eyes were the colour of a summer sky.   And John Broom felt as he had felt when he first saw Miss Betty's cockatoo.

In repose the Highlander's eye was as clear as a cairn-gorm and as cold, but when it fell upon John Broom it took a twinkle not quite unlike the twinkle in the one eye of the sailor; and then, to his amazement, this grand creature beckoned to John Broom with a rather dirty hand.

" Yes, sir," said John Broom, staring up at the spendid giant, with eyes of wonder.

" I'm saying," said the Highlander, confidentially (and it had a pleasant homely sound to hear him speak like the farm-bailiff)—" I'm saying, I'm confined to barracks, ye ken ; and I'll gie' ye a hawpenny if ye'll get the bottle filled wi' whusky.   Roun' yon corner ye'll see the ' Britain's Defenders.' "

But at this moment he erected himself, his turquoise eyes looked straight before them, and he put his hand to his head and moved it slowly away again, as a young man with more swinging grandeur of colours and fur and plumes, and with greater glitterings of gems and silver, passed by, a sword clattering after him.

Meanwhile John Broom had been round the corner and was back again,

" What for are ye stannin' there, ye fule ? " asked his new friend.   " What for didna ye gang for the whusky ? "

" It's here, sir."

" My certy, ye dinna let the grass grow under your feet," said the Highlander ; and he added, " If ye want to run errands, laddie, ye can come back again."

It was the beginning of a fresh life for John Broom. With many other idle or homeless boys he now haunted the barracks, and ran errands for the soldiers.   His fleetness of foot and ready wit made him the favourite. Perhaps, too, his youth and his bright face and eyes pleaded for him, for British soldiers are a tender-hearted race.

He was knocked about, but never cruelly, and he got plenty of coppers and broken victuals, and now and then an old cap or pair of boots, a world too large for him. His principal errands were to fetch liquor for the soldiers. In arms and pockets he would sometimes carry a dozen bottles at once, and fly back from the canteen or public-house without breaking one.

Before the summer was over he was familiar with every barrack-room and guard-room in the place; he had food to eat and coppers to spare, and he shared his bits with the mongrel dogs who lived, as he did, on the good-nature of the garrison.

It must be confessed that neatness was not among John Broom's virtues. He looped his rags together with bits of string, and wasted his pence or lost them. The soldiers standing at the bar would often give him a drink out of their pewter-pots. It choked him at first, and then he got used to it, and liked it. Some relics of Miss Betty's teaching kept him honest. He would not condescend to sip by the way out of the soldiers' jugs and bottles as other errand-boys did, but he came to feel rather proud of laying his twopence on the counter, and emptying his own pot of beer with a grimace to the bystanders through the glass at the bottom.

One day he was winking through the froth of a pint of porter at the canteen sergeant's daughter, who was in fits of laughing, when the pewter was knocked out of his grasp, and the big Highlander's hand was laid on his shoulder and bore him twenty or thirty yards from the place in one swoop.

"I'll trouble ye to give me your attention," said the Highlander, when they came to a standstill, "and to speak the truth. Did ye ever see me the worse of liquor?"

John Broom had several remembrances of the clearest kind to that effect, so he put up his arms to shield his head from the probable blow, and said, "Yes, M'Alister."

"How often?" asked the Scotchman.
"I never counted," said John Broom; "pretty often."

"How many good-conduct stripes do you ken me to have lost of your ain knowledge?"

"Three, M'Alister."

"Is there a finer man than me in the regiment?" asked the Highlander, drawing up his head.

"That there's not," said John Broom, warmly.

"Our sairgent, now," drawled the Scotchman, "wad ye say he was a better man than me?"

"Nothing like so good," said John Broom, sincerely.

"And what d'ye suppose, man," said the Highlander, firing with sudden passion, till the light of his clear blue eyes seemed to pierce John Broom's very soul—"what d'ye suppose has hindered me that I'm not sairgent, when yon man is? What has keepit me from being an officer, that had served my country in twa battles when oor quartermaster hadna enlisted? Wha gets my money? What lost me my stripes? What loses me decent folks' respect and, waur than that, my ain? What gars a hand that can grip a broadsword tremble like a woman's? What fills the canteen and the kirkyard? What robs a man of health and wealth and peace? What ruins weans and women, and makes mair homes desolate than war? Drink, man, drink! The deevil of drink!"

It was not till the glare in his eyes had paled that John Broom ventured to speak. Then he said,—

"Why don't ye give it up, M'Alister?"

The man rose to his full height, and laid his hand heavily on the boy's shoulder, and his eyes seemed to fade with that pitiful, weary look, which only such blue eyes show so well, "Because I *canna*," said he; "because, for as big as I am, I canna. But for as little as you are, laddie, ye can, and, Heaven help me, ye shall."

That evening he called John Broom into the barrack-room where he slept. He was sitting on the edge of his bed, and had a little wooden money-box in his hands.

"What money have ye, laddie?" he asked.

John Broom pulled out three halfpence lately earned, and the Scotchman dropped them slowly into the box. Then he turned the key, and put it into his pocket, and gave the box to the boy.

"Ye'll put what ye earn in there," said he, "I'll keep the key, and ye'll keep the box yoursel; and when it's opened we'll open it together, and lay out your savings in decent clothes for ye against the winter."

At this moment some men passing to the canteen, shouted, "M'Alister!" The Highlander did not answer, but he started to the door. Then he stood irresolute, and then turned and reseated himself.

"Gang and bring me a bit o' tobacco," he said, giving John Broom a penny. And when the boy had gone he emptied his pocket of the few pence left, and dropped them into the box, muttering, "If he manna, I wunna."

And when the tobacco came, he lit his pipe, and sat on the bench outside, and snarled at every one who spoke to him.

OUTPOST DUTY.—THE SERGEANT'S STORY.—GRAND ROUNDS.

It was a bitterly cold winter. The soldiers drank a great deal, and John Broom was constantly trotting up and down, and the box grew very heavy.

Bottles were filled and refilled, in spite of greatly increased strictness in the discipline of the garrison, for there were rumours of invasion, and penalties were heavy, and sentry posts were increased, and the regiments were kept in readiness for action.

The Highlander had not cured himself of drinking, though he had cured John Broom. But, like others, he was more wary just now, and had hitherto escaped the heavy punishments inflicted in a time of probable war; and John Broom watched over him with the fidelity of a sheep dog, and more than once had roused him with a can of cold water when he was all but caught by his superiors in a state of stupor, which would not have been credited to the frost alone.

The talk of invasion had become grave, when one day a body of men were ordered for outpost duty, and M'Alister was among them. The officer had got a room for them in a farmhouse, where they sat round the fire, and went out by turns to act as sentries at various posts for an hour or two at a time.

The novelty was delightful to John Broom. He hung about the farmhouse, and warmed himself at the soldiers' fire.

In the course of the day M'Alister got him apart, and whispered, " I'm going on duty the night at ten, laddie. It's fearsome cold, and I hav'na had a drop to warm me the day. If ye could ha' brought me a wee drappie to the corner of the three roads—it's twa miles from here, I'm thinking——"

" It's not the miles, M'Alister," said John Broom, "but you're on outpost duty, and——"

" And you're misdoubting what may be done to ye for bringing liquor to a sentry on duty? Aye, aye, lad, ye do weel to be cautious," said the Highlander, and he turned away.

But it was not the fear of consequences to himself which had made John Broom hesitate, and he was stung by the implication.

The night was dark and very cold, and the Highlander had been pacing up and down his post for about half-an-hour, when his quick ear caught a faint sound of footsteps.

" Wha goes there ? " said he.

" It's I, M'Alister," whispered John Broom.

"Whisht, laddie," said the sentry; "are ye there after all? Did no one see ye?"

" Not a soul; I crept by the hedges. Here's your whisky, M'Alister; but oh be careful!" said the lad.

The Scotchman's eyes glittered greedily at the bottle.

" Never fear," said he, " I'll just rub a wee drappie on the pawms of my hands to keep away the frost-bite, for it's awsome cold, man. Now away wi' ye, and take tent, laddie, keep off the other sentries."

John Broom went back as carefully as he had come, and slipped in to warm himself by the guard-room fire.

It was a good one, and the soldiers sat close round it. The officer was writing a letter in another room, and in a low, impressive voice, the sergeant was telling a story which was listened to with breathless attention. John Broom was fond of stories, and he listened also.

It was of a friend of the sergeant's, who had been a boy with him in the same village at home, who had seen active service with him abroad, and who had slept at his post on such a night as this, from the joint effects of cold and drink. It was war time, and he had been tried by court-martial, and shot for the offence. The sergeant had been one of the firing party to execute his friend, and they had taken leave of each other as brothers, before the final parting face to face in this last awful scene.

The man's voice was faltering, when the tale was cut short by the jingling of the field officer's accoutrements as he rode by to visit the outposts. In an instant the officer and men turned out to receive him; and, after the usual formalities, he rode on. The officer went back to his letter, and the sergeant and his men to their fireside.

The opening of the doors had let in a fresh volume of cold, and one of the men called to John Broom to mend the fire. But he was gone.

    *   *   *   *   *   *   *

John Broom was fleet of foot, and there are certain moments which lift men beyond their natural powers, but he had set himself a hard task.

As he listened to the sergeant's tale, an agonising fear smote him for his friend M'Alister. Was there any hope that the Highlander could keep himself from the whisky? Officers were making their rounds at very short intervals just now, and if drink and cold overcame him at his post!

Close upon these thoughts came the jingling of the field officer's sword, and the turn out of the guard. "Who goes there?"—"Rounds."—"What rounds?"—"Grand rounds." "Halt, grand rounds, advance one, and give the counter-sign!" The familiar words struck coldly on John Broom's heart, as if they had been orders to a firing party, and the bandage was already across the Highlander's blue eyes.

Would the grand rounds be challenged at the three roads to-night ?   He darted out into the snow.

He flew, as the crow flies, across the fields, to where M‘Alister was on duty.   It was a much shorter distance than by the road, which was winding ; but whether this would balance the difference between a horse's pace and his own was the question, and there being no time to question, he ran on.

He kept his black head down, and ran from his shoulders. The clatter, clatter, jingle, jingle, on the hard road came to him through the still frost on a level with his left ear.   It was terrible, but he held on, dodging under the hedges to be out of sight, and the sound lessened, and by-and-by, the road having wound about, he could hear it faintly, *but behind him.*

And he reached the three roads, and M‘Alister was asleep in the ditch.

But when, with jingle and clatter, the field officer of the day reached the spot, the giant Highlander stood like a watch-tower at his post, with a little snow on the black plumes that drooped upon his shoulders.

HOSPITAL.—" HAME."

John Broom did not see the Highlander again for two or three days.   It was Christmas week, and, in spite of the war panic, there was festivity enough in the barracks to keep the errand-boy very busy.

Then came New Year's Eve—" Hogmenay," as the Scotch call it—and it was the Highland regiment's particular festival.   Worn-out with whisky-fetching and with helping to deck barrack-rooms and carrying pots and trestles, John Broom was having a nap in the evening, in company with a mongrel deer-hound, when a man shook

him, and said, " I heard some one asking for ye an hour or
two back ; M'Alister wants ye."

" Where is he ? " said John Broom, jumping to his feet.

" In hospital ; he's been there a day or two. He got
cold on out-post duty, and its flown to his lungs, they say.
Ye see he's been a hard drinker, has M'Alister, and I
expect he's breaking up."

With which very just conclusion the speaker went on
into the canteen, and John Broom ran to the hospital.

Stripped of his picturesque trappings, and with no
plumes to shadow the hollows in his temples, M'Alister
looked gaunt and feeble enough, as he lay in the little
hospital bed, which barely held his long limbs. Such a
wreck of giant powers of body, and noble qualities of
mind as the drink-shops are preparing for the hospitals
every day !

Since the quickly-reached medical decision that he was
in a rapid decline, and that nothing could be done for him,
M'Alister had been left a good deal alone. His intellect
(and it was no fool's intellect,) was quite clear, and if the
long hours by himself, in which he reckoned with his own
soul, had hastened the death-damps on his brow, they had
also written there an expression which was new to John
Broom. It was not the old sour look, it was a kind of
noble gravity.

His light-blue eyes brightened as the boy came in, and
he held out his hand, and John Broom took it with both
his, saying—

" I never heard till this minute, M'Alister. Eh, I do
hope you'll be better soon."

" The Lord being merciful to me," said the Highlander.
" But *this* warld's nearly past, laddie, and I was fain to see
ye again. Dinna greet, man, for I've important business
wi' ye, and I should wish your attention. Firstly, I'm
aboot to hand ower to ye the key of your box. Tak it,

and put it in a pocket that's no got a hole in it, if you're worth one. Secondly, there's a bit bag I made mysel', and it's got a trifle o' money in it that I'm giving and bequeathing to ye, under certain conditions, namely, that ye shall spend the contents of the box according to my last wishes and instructions, with the ultimate end of your ain benefit, ye'll understand."

A fit of coughing here broke M'Alister's discourse ; but, after drinking from a cup beside him, he put aside John Broom's remonstrances with a dignified movement of his hand, and continued,—

" When a body comes of decent folk, he won't just care, maybe, to have their names brought up in a barrack-room. Ye never heard me say ought of my father or my mither ? "

" Never, M'Alister."

" I'd a good hame," said the Highlander, with a decent pride in his tone. " It was a strict hame—I've no cause now to deceive mysel', and I'm thinking it was a wee bit ower strict—but it was a good hame. I left it, man—I ran away."

The glittering blue eyes turned sharply on the lad, and he went on :—

" A body doesna' care to turn his byeganes oot for every fool to peck at. Did I ever speer about your past life, and whar ye came from ? "

" Never, M'Alister."

" But that's no to say that, if I knew manners, I didna obsairve. And there's been things now and again, John Broom, that's gar'd me think that ye've had what I had, and done as I did. Did ye rin awa', laddie ? "

John Broom nodded his black head, but tears choked his voice.

" Man ! " said the Highlander, " ane word's as gude's a thousand. Gang back ! Gang hame ! There's the bit siller here that's to tak ye, and the love yonder that's waiting ye. Listen to a dying man, laddie, and gang hame ! "

M

"I doubt if they'd have me," sobbed John Broom, "I gave 'em a deal of trouble, M'Alister."

"And d'ye think, lad, that that thought has na' cursed *me*, and keepit me from them that loved me? Aye lad, and till this week I never overcame it."

"Weel may I want to save ye, bairn," added the Highlander tenderly, "for it was the thocht of a' ye riskit for the like of me at the three roads, that made me consider wi' mysel' that I've aiblins been turning my back a' my wilfu' life on love that's bigger than a man's deservings. It's near done now, and it'll never lie in my poor power so much as rightly to thank ye. It's strange that a man should set store by a good name that he doesn' deserve; but if ony blessings of mine could bring ye good, they're yours, that saved an old soldier's honour, and let him die respectit in his regiment."

"Oh, M'Alister, let me fetch one of the chaplains to write a letter to fetch your father," cried John Broom.

"The minister's been here this morning," said the Highlander, "and I've tell't him mair than I've tell't you. And he's jest directed me to put my sinful trust in the Father of us a'. I've sinned heaviest against *Him*, laddie, but His love is stronger than the lave."

John Broom remained by his friend, whose painful fits of coughing, and of gasping for breath, were varied by intervals of seeming stupor. When a candle had been brought in and placed near the bed, the Highlander roused himself and asked,—

"Is there a Bible on yon table? Could ye read a bit to me, laddie?"

There is little need to dwell on the bitterness of heart with which John Broom confessed,—

"I can't read big words, M'Alister."

"Did ye never go to school?" said the Scotchman.

"I didn't learn," said the poor boy; "I played."

"Aye, aye. Weel, ye'll learn, when he gang hame," said the Highlander, in gentle tones.

"I'll never get home," said John Broom, passionately. "I'll never forgive myself. I'll never get over it, that I couldn't read to ye when ye wanted me, M'Alister."

"Gently, gently," said the Scotchman. "Dinna daunt yoursel' owermuch wi' the past, laddie. And for me— I'm not that presoomtious to think I can square up a misspent life as a man might compound wi's creditors. 'Gin HE forgi'es me, He'll forgi'e; but it's not a prayer up or a chapter doun that'll stan' between me and the Almighty. So dinna fret yoursel', but let me think while I may.

And so, far into the night, the Highlander lay silent, and John Broom watched by him.

It was just midnight when he partly raised himself, and cried,—

"Whisht, laddie! do ye hear the pipes?"

The dying ears must have been quick, for John Broom heard nothing; but in a few moments he heard the bag-pipes from the officers' mess, where they were keeping Hogmenay. They were playing the old year out with "Auld lang syne," and the Highlander beat the tune out with his hand, and his eyes gleamed out of his rugged face in the dim light, as cairngorms glitter in dark tartan.

There was a pause after the first verse, and he grew restless, and turning doubtfully to where John Broom sat, as if his sight were failing, he said, "Ye'll mind your promise, ye'll gang hame?" And after awhile he repeated the last word,

"*Hame!*"

But as he spoke there settled over his face a smile so tender and so full of happiness, that John Broom held his breath as he watched him. As the light of sunrise creeps over the face of some rugged rock, it crept from chin to brow, and the pale blue eyes shone tranquil, like water that reflects heaven.

And when it had passed it left them still open, but gems that had lost their ray.

LUCK GOES.—AND COMES AGAIN.

The spirit does not always falter in its faith because the flesh is weary with hope deferred. When week after week, month after month, and year after year, went by and John Broom was not found, the disappointment seemed to "age" the little ladies, as Thomasina phrased it. But yet they said to the parson, "We do not regret it."

"GOD forbid that you should regret it," said he.

And even the lawyer (whose heart was kinder than his tongue) abstained from taunting them with his prophecies, and said, "The force of the habits of early education is a power as well as that of inherent tendencies. It is only for your sake that I regret a too romantic benevolence." And Miss Betty and Miss Kitty tried to put the matter quite away. But John Broom was very closely bound up with the life of many years past. Thomasina mourned him as if he had been her son, and Thomasina being an old and valuable servant, it is needless to say that when she was miserable no one in the house was permitted to be quite at ease.

As to Pretty Cocky, he lived, but Miss Kitty fancied that he grew less pretty and drooped upon his polished perch.

There were times when the parson felt almost conscience-stricken because he had encouraged the adoption of John Broom. Disappointments fall heavily upon elderly people. They may submit better than the young, but they do not so easily revive. The little old ladies looked greyer and more nervous, and the little old house looked greyer and gloomier than of old.

Indeed there were other causes of anxiety. Times were changing, prices were rising, and the farm did not thrive. The lawyer said that the farm-bailiff neglected his duties, and that the cowherd did nothing but drink ; but Miss Betty trembled, and said they could not part with old servants.

The farm-bailiff had his own trouble, but he kept it to himself. No one knew how severely he had beaten John Broom the day before he ran away, but he remembered it himself with painful clearness. Harsh men are apt to have consciences, and his was far from easy about the lad who had been entrusted to his care. He could not help thinking of it when the day's work was over, and he had to keep filling up his evening whisky-glass again and again to drown disagreeable thoughts.

The whisky answered this purpose, but it made him late in the morning; it complicated business on market days, not to the benefit of the farm, and it put him at a disadvantage in dealing with the drunken cowherd.

The cowherd was completely upset by John Broom's mysterious disappearance, and he comforted himself as the farm-bailiff did, but to a larger extent. And Thomasina winked at many irregularities in consideration of the groans of sympathy with which he responded to her tears as they sat round the hearth where John Broom no longer lay.

At the time that he vanished from Lingborough the gossips of the country side said, " This comes of making pets of tramps' brats, when honest folks' sons may toil and moil without notice." But when it was proved that the tramp-boy had stolen nothing, when all search for him was vain, and when prosperity faded from the place season by season and year by year, there were old folk who whispered that the gaudily-clothed child Miss Betty had found under

the broom-bush had something more than common in him,
and that whoever and whatever had offended the eerie
creature, he had taken the luck of Lingborough with him
when he went away.

It was early summer. The broom was shining in the
hedges with uncommon wealth of golden blossoms. " The
lanes look for all the world as they did the year that poor
child was found," said Thomasina, wiping her eyes. Annie
the lass sobbed hysterically, and the cowherd found himself
so low in spirits that after gazing dismally at the cow-stalls,
which had not been cleaned for days past, he betook himself
to the ale-house to refresh his energies for this and other
arrears of work.

On returning to the farm, however, he found his hands
still feeble, and he took a drop or two more to steady them,
after which it occured to him that certain new potatoes
which he had had orders to dig were yet in the ground.
The wood was not chopped for the next day's use, and he
wondered what had become of a fork he had had in the
morning and had laid down somewhere.

So he seated himself on some straw in the corner to
think about it all, and whilst he was thinking he fell fast
asleep.

By his own account many remarkable things had befallen
him in the course of his life, including that meeting with a
Black Something to which allusion has been made, but
nothing so strange as what happened to him that night.

When he awoke in the morning and sat up on the straw,
and looked around him, the stable was freshly cleaned, the
litter in the stalls was shaken and turned, and near the
door was an old barrel of newly-dug potatoes, and the fork
stood by it. And when he ran to the wood-house there lay
the wood neatly chopped and piled to take away.

He kept his own counsel that day and took credit for
the work, but when on the morrow the farm-bailiff was at

a loss to know who had thinned the turnips that were left to do in the upper field, and Annie the lass found the kitchen-cloths she had left overnight to soak, rubbed through and rinsed, and laid to dry, the cowherd told his tale to Thomasina, and begged for a bowl of porridge and cream to set in the barn, as one might set a mouse-trap baited with cheese.

"For," said he, "the luck of Lingborough's come back, missis. *It's Lob Lie-by-the-fire!*"

LOB LIE-BY-THE-FIRE.

"It's Lob Lie-by-the-fire!"

So Thomasina whispered exultingly, and Annie the lass timidly. Thomasina cautioned the cowherd to hold his tongue, and she said nothing to the little ladies on the subject. She felt certain that they would tell the parson, and he might not approve. The farm-bailiff knew of a farm on the Scotch side of the Border where a Brownie had been driven away by the minister preaching his last Sunday's sermon over again at him, and as Thomasina said, "There'd been little enough luck at Lingborough lately, that they should wish to scare it away when it came."

And yet the news leaked out gently, and was soon known all through the neighbourhood—as a secret.

"The luck of Lingborough's come back. Lob's lying by the fire!"

He could be heard at his work any night, and several people had seen him, though this vexed Thomasina, who knew well that the Good People do not like to be watched at their labours.

The cowherd had not been able to resist peeping down through chinks in the floor of the loft above the barn, where he slept, and one night he had seen Lob fetching straw for the cowhouse. "A great rough, black fellow," said he, and he certainly grew bigger and rougher and blacker every time the cowherd told the tale.

The Lubber-fiend appeared next to a boy who was loitering at a late hour somewhere near the little ladies' kitchen-garden, and whom he pursued and pelted with

mud till the lad nearly lost his wits with terror. (It was the same boy who was put in the lock-up in the autumn for stealing Farmer Mangel's Siberian crabs.)

For this trick, however, the rough elf stoned by leaving three pecks of newly-gathered fruit in the kitchen the following morning. Never had there been such a pre-serving season at Lingborough within the memory of Thomasina.

The truth is, hobgoblins, from Puck to Will-o'-the-wisp

are apt to play practical jokes and knock people about
whom they meet after sunset.   A dozen tales of such were
rife, and folks were more amused than amazed by Lob Lie-
by-the-fire's next prank.

There was an aged pauper who lived on the charity of
the little ladies, and whom it was Miss Betty's practice to
employ to do light weeding in the fields for heavy wages.
This venerable person was toddling to his home in the
gloaming with a barrow-load of Miss Betty's new potatoes,
dexterously hidden by an upper sprinkling of groundsel
and hemlock, when the Lubber-fiend sprang out from
behind an elder-bush, ran at the old man with his black
head, and knocked him, heels uppermost, into the ditch.
The wheelbarrow was afterwards found in Miss Betty's
farm-yard, quite empty.

And when the cowherd (who had his own opinion of the
aged pauper, and it was a very poor one) went that evening
to drink Lob Lie-by-the-fire's health from a bottle he kept
in the harness-room window, he was nearly choked with the
contents, which had turned into salt and water, as fairy
jewels turn to withered leaves.

But luck had come to Lingborough.   There had not
been such crops for twice seven years past.

The lay-away hen's eggs were brought regularly to the
kitchen.

The ducklings were not eaten by rats.

No fowls were stolen.

The tub of pig-meal lasted three times as long as usual.

The cart-wheels and gate-hinges were oiled by unseen
fingers.

The mushrooms in the croft gathered themselves and
lay down on a dish in the larder.

It is by small savings that a farm thrives, and Miss
Betty's farm throve.

Everybody worked with more alacrity.   Annie the lass

said the butter came in a way that made it a pleasure to churn.

The neighbours knew even more than those on the spot. They said—That since Lob came back to Lingborough the hens laid eggs as large as turkeys' eggs, and the turkeys' eggs, were—oh, you wouldn't believe the size!

That the cows gave nothing but cream, and that Thomasina skimmed butter off it as less lucky folk skim cream from milk.

That her cheeses were as rich as butter.

That she sold all she made, for Lob took the fairy butter from the old trees in the avenue, and made it up into pats for Miss Betty's table.

That if you bought Lingborough turnips, you might feed your cows on them all the winter and the milk would be as sweet as new-mown hay.

That horses foddered on Lingborough hay would have thrice the strength of others, and that sheep who cropped Lingborough pastures would grow three times as fat.

That for as good a watch-dog as it was, the sheep dog never barked at Lob, a plain proof that he was more than human.

That for all its good luck it was not safe to loiter near the place after dark, if you wished to keep your senses. And if you took so much as a fallen apple belonging to Miss Betty, you might look out for palsy or St. Vitus's dance, or be carried off bodily to the underground folk.

Finally, that it was well all the cows gave double, for that Lob Lie-by-the-fire drank two gallons of the best cream every day, with curds, porridge, and other dainties to match. But what did that matter, when he had been overheard to swear that luck should not leave Lingborough till Miss Betty owned half the country side?

Miss Betty is Surprised.

Miss Betty and Miss Kitty having accepted a polite invitation from Mrs. General Dunmaw, went down to tea with that lady one fine evening in this eventful summer.

Death had made a gap or two in the familiar circle during the last fourteen years, but otherwise it was quite the same, except that the lawyer was married and not quite so sarcastic, and that Mrs. Brown Jasey had brought a young niece with her dressed in the latest fashion, which looked quite as odd as new fashions are wont to do, and with a *coiffure* " enough to frighten the French away," as her aunt told her.

It was while this young lady was getting more noise out of Mrs. Dunmaw's red silk and rosewood piano than had been shaken out of it during the last thirty years, that the lawyer brought his cup of coffee to Miss Betty's side, and said, suavely, " I hear wonderful accounts of Lingborough, dear Miss Betty."

" I am thankful to say, sir, that the farm is doing well this year. I am very thankful, for the past few years have been unfavourable, and we had begun to face the fact that it might be necessary to sell the old place. And, I will not deny, sir, that it would have gone far to break my heart, to say nothing of my sister Kitty's."

" Oh, we shouldn't have let it come to that," said the lawyer, " I could have raised a loan——"

" Sir," said Miss Betty with dignity, " if we have our own pride, I hope it's an honest one. Lingborough will have passed out of our family when it's kept up on borrowed money."

" I *could* live in lodgings," added Miss Betty, firmly, " little as I've been accustomed to it, but *not in debt.*"

" Well, well, my dear madam, we needn't talk about it now. But I'm dying of curiosity as to the mainstay of all this good luck."

"That the lawyer brought his cup of coffee to Miss Betty's side."

"The turnips——" began Miss Betty.

"Bless my soul, Miss Betty!" cried the lawyer, "I'm not talking of turnips. I'm talking of Lob Lie-by-the-fire, as all the country side is for that matter."

"The country people have plenty of tales of him," said Miss Betty, with some pride in the family goblin. "He used to haunt the old barns, they say, in my great-grandfather's time."

"And now you've got him back again," said the lawyer.

"Not that I know of," said Miss Betty.

On which the lawyer poured into her astonished ear all the latest news on the subject, and if it had lost nothing before reaching his house in the town, it rather gained in marvels as he repeated it to Miss Betty.

No wonder that the little lady was anxious to get home to question Thomasina, and that somewhat before the usual hour she said,—

"Sister Kitty, if it's not too soon for the servant——"

And the parson, threading his way to where Mrs Dunmaw's china crape shawl (dyed crimson) shone in the bow window, said, "The clergy should keep respectable hours, madam; especially when they are as old as I am. Will you allow me to thank you for a very pleasant evening, and to say good-night?"

THE PARSON AND THE LUBBER-FIEND.

"Do you think there'd be any harm in leaving it alone, sister Betty?" said Miss Kitty, tremulously.

They had reached Lingborough, and the parson had come in with them, by Miss Betty's request, and Thomasina had been duly examined.

"Eh, Miss Betty, why should ye chase away good luck with the minister?" cried she.

“Sister Kitty! Thomasina!” said Miss Betty. “I would, not accept good luck from a doubtful quarter to save Lingborough. But if It can face this excellent clergyman the Being who haunted my great grandfather's farm is still welcome to the old barns, and you, Thomasina, need not grudge It cream or curds.”

“You're quite right, sister Betty,” said Miss Kitty. “You always are; but oh dear, oh dear!”—

“Thomasina tells me,” said Miss Betty, turning to the parson, “that on chilly evenings It sometimes comes and lies by the kitchen fire after they have gone to bed, and I can distinctly remember my grandmother mentioning the same thing. Thomasina has of late left the kitchen door on the latch for Its convenience, and as they had to sit up late for us, she and Annie have taken their work into the still-room to leave the kitchen free for Lob Lie-by-the-fire. They have not looked into the kitchen this evening, as such beings do not like to be watched. But they fancy that they heard It come in. I trust, sir, that neither in myself nor my sister Kitty does timidity exceed a proper feminine sensibility, where duty is concerned. If you will be good enough to precede us, we will go to meet the old friend of my great grandfather's fortunes, and we leave it entirely to your valuable discretion to pursue what course you think proper on the occasion.”

“Is this the door?” said the parson, cheerfully, after knocking his head against black beams and just saving his legs down shallow and unexpected steps on his way to the kitchen—beams so unfelt and steps so familiar to the women that it had never struck them that the long passage was not the most straightforward walk a man could take— “I think you said It generally lies on the hearth?”

The happy thought struck Thomasina that the parson might be frightened out of his unlucky interference.

“Aye, aye, sir,” said she from behind. “We've heard

him rolling by the fire, and growling like thunder to himself.   They say he's an awful size, too, with the strength of four men, and a long tail, and eyes like coals of fire."

But Thomasina spoke in vain, for the parson opened the door, and as they pressed in, the moonlight streaming through the latticed window showed Lob lying by the fire.

"There's his tail! Ay——k!" screeched Annie the lass, and away she went, without drawing breath, to the top garret, where she locked and bolted herself in, and sat her bandbox flat, and screamed for help.

But it was the plumy tail of the sheep dog, who was lying there with the Lubber-fiend.   And Lob was asleep, with his arms round the sheep dog's neck, and the sheep dog's head lay on his breast, and his own head touched the dog's.

And it was a smaller head than the parson had been led to expect, and it had thick black hair.

As the parson bent over the hearth, Thomasina took Miss Kitty round the waist, and Miss Betty clutched her black velvet bag till the steel beads ran into her hands, and they were quite prepared for an explosion, and sulphur, and blue lights, and thunder.

And then the parson's deep round voice broke the silence, saying,—

"Is that you lad? GOD bless you, John Broom. You're welcome home!"

THE END.

Some things—such as gossip—gain in the telling, but there are others before which words fail, though each heart knows its own power of sympathy.   And such was the joy of the little ladies and of Thomasina at John Broom's return.

The sheep dog had had his satisfaction out long ago,

and had kept it to himself, but how Pretty Cocky crowed, and chuckled, and danced, and bowed his crest, and covered his face with his amber wings, and kicked his seed-pot over, and spilled his water-pot on to the Derbyshire marble chess-table, and screamed till the room rang again, and went on screaming, with Miss Kitty's pocket-hankerchief over his head to keep him quiet, my poor pen can but imperfectly describe.

The desire to atone for the past which had led John Broom to act the part of one of those Good-fellows who have, we must fear, finally deserted us, will be easily understood.   And to a nature of his type, the earning of some self-respect, and of a new character before others, was perhaps a necessary prelude to future well-doing.

He did do well. He became "a good scholar," as farmers were then. He spent as much of his passionate energies on the farm as the farm would absorb, and he restrained the rest. It is not cockatoos only who have sometimes to live and be happy in this unfinished life with one wing clipped.

In fine weather, when the perch was put into the garden, Miss Betty was sometimes startled by stumbling on John Broom in the dusk, sitting on his heels, the unfastened chain in his hand, with his black head lovingly laid against Cocky's white and yellow poll, talking in a low voice, and apparently with the sympathy of his companion ; and, as Miss Betty justly feared, of that "other side of the world," which they both knew, and which both at times had cravings to revisit.

Even after the sobering influences of middle age had touched him, and a wife and children bound him with the quiet ties of home, he had (at long intervals) his "restless times," when his good "missis" would bring out a little store laid by in one of the children's socks, and would bid him "Be off, and get a breath of the sea-air," but on con-

N

dition that the sock went with him as his purse. John Broom always looked ashamed to go, but he came back the better, and his wife was quite easy in his absence with that confidence in her knowledge of "the master," which is so mysterious to the unmarried, and which Miss Betty looked upon as "want of feeling" to the end. She always dreaded that he would not return, and a little ruse which she adopted of giving him money to make bargains for foreign articles of *vertu* with the sailors, is responsible for many of the choicest ornaments in the Lingborough parlour.

"The sock'll bring him home," said Mrs. Broom, and home he came, and never could say what he had been doing. Nor was the account given by Thomasina's cousin, who was a tide-waiter down yonder, particularly satisfying to the women's curiosity. He said that John Broom was always about; that he went aboard of all the craft in the bay, and asked whence they came and whither they were bound. That, being once taunted to it, he went up the rigging of a big vessel like a cat, and came down it looking like a fool. That, as a rule, he gossipped and shared his tobacco with sailors and fishermen, and brought out the sock much oftener than was prudent for the benefit of the ragged boys who haunt the quay.

He had two other weaknesses, which a faithful biographer must chronicle.

A regiment on the march would draw him from the plough-tail itself, and "With daddy to see the pretty soldiers" was held to excuse any of Mrs. Broom's children from household duties.

The other shall be described in the graphic language of that acute observer the farm-bailiff.

"If there cam' an Irish beggar, wi' a stripy cloot roond him and a bellows under 's arm, and ca'd himsel' a Hielander, the lad wad gi'e him his silly head off his shoulders."

As to the farm-bailiff, perhaps no one felt more or said less than he did on John Broom's return. But the tones of his voice had tender associations for the boy's ears as he took off his speckled hat, and after contemplating the inside for some moments, put it on again, and said,—

"Aweel, lad, sae ye've cam' hame?"

But he listened with quivering face when John Broom told the story of M'Alister, and when it was ended he rose and went out, and "took the pledge" against drink, and—kept it.

Moved by similar enthusiasm, the cowherd took the pledge also, and if he didn't keep it, he certainly drank less, chiefly owing to the vigilant oversight of the farm-bailiff, who now exercised his natural severity almost exclusively in the denunciation of all liquors whatsoever, from the cowherd's whisky to Thomasina's elder-flower wine.

The plain cousin left his money to the little old ladies, and Lingborough continued to flourish.

Partly perhaps because of this, it is doubtful if John Broom was ever looked upon by the rustics as quite "like other folk."

The favourite version of his history is that he was Lob under the guise of a child; that he was driven away by new clothes; that he returned from unwillingness to see an old family go to ruin "which he had served for hundreds of years;" that the parson preached his last Sunday's sermon at him; and that, having stood that test, he took his place among Christian people.

Whether a name invented off-hand, however plain and sensible, does not stick to a man as his father's does, is a question. But John Broom was not often called by his.

With Scotch caution, the farm-bailiff seldom exceeded the safe title of "Man!" and the parson was apt to address him as "My dear boy" when he had certainly outgrown the designation.

Miss Betty called him John Broom, but the people called him by the name he had earned.

And long after his black hair lay white and thick on his head, like snow on the old barn roof, and when his dark eyes were dim in an honoured old age, the village children would point him out to each other, crying, "There goes Lob Lie-by-the-fire, the Luck of Lingborough!"